# A SILO STORY
# FIRST SHIFT
## LEGACY

**BY HUGH HOWEY**

# First Shift:
# Legacy

Copyright © 2012 by Hugh Howey

All rights reserved. No part of this book may be reproduced in any form by any electronic or mechanical means including photocopying, recording, or information storage and retrieval without permission in writing from the author.

Edited by Lisa Kelly-Wilson, Dr. Amber Lyda, and David Gatewood
Cover design by Jerry Aman, Mike Tabor, and John Jarrett
Interior design and layout by Hugh Howey

ISBN-13: 978-1475154771
ISBN-10: 1-47515477-1

www.hughhowey.com

Give feedback on the book at:
hughhowey@gmail.com
Twitter: @hughhowey

Printed in the U.S.A

For Tongjai and Andy Bell
Together Forever

*In 2007, the Center for Automation in Nanobiotech (CAN) outlined the hardware and software platform that would one day allow robots smaller than human cells to make medical diagnoses, conduct repairs, and even self-propagate.*

*In the same year, the CBS network re-aired a program about the effects of propranolol on sufferers of extreme trauma. A simple pill, it had been discovered, could wipe out the memory of any traumatic event.*

*At almost the same moment in humanity's broad history, mankind had discovered the means for bringing about its utter downfall. And the ability to forget it ever happened.*

# Prologue
## 2110 • Beneath the hills of Fulton County, Georgia

Troy returned to the living and found himself inside of a tomb. He awoke to a world of confinement, a thick sheet of frosted glass pressed near to his face.

Dark shapes stirred on the other side of the icy murk. He tried to lift his arms, to beat on the glass, but his muscles were too weak. He attempted to scream—but could only cough. The taste in his mouth was foul. His ears rang with the clank of heavy locks opening, the hiss of air, the squeak of hinges long dormant.

The lights overhead were bright, the hands on him warm. They helped him sit while he continued to cough, his breath clouding the chill air. Someone had water. Pills to take. The water was cool, the pills bitter. Troy fought down a few gulps. He was unable to hold the glass without help, hands trembling, memories flooding back, scenes from long nightmares. The feeling of deep time and yesterdays mingled. He shivered. The pills hit his gut, and his grip on the memories seemed to loosen.

A paper gown. The sting of tape removed. A tug on his arm, a tube pulled from his groin. Two men dressed in white helped him out. Steam rose all around him, air condensing and dispersing like dreams upon waking.

His legs were that of a foal's, working at birth but not well. Blinking against the glare, exercising lids long shut, Troy saw the rows of coffins full of the living that stretched toward the distant and curved walls. The ceiling felt low; there was the suffocating press of dirt stacked high above. All that dirt and the dead, stacked high. And the years. So many years had passed. Anyone he cared about would be gone.

Everything was gone.

The pills were bitter in Troy's throat. He tried to swallow. The memories were fading. He was going to lose anything bad he'd ever known.

He collapsed—but the men in the white coveralls saw this coming. They caught him and lowered him to the ground, a paper gown rustling on shivering skin.

Memories flooded back before fading; recollections rained down like bombs and then were gone. Awareness came—however fleeting.

The pills could only do so much. It took time to destroy the past. Until then, the nightmares were vivid and with him.

Troy sobbed into his palms, a sympathetic hand resting on his head. The two men in white gifted him with quiet and calm. They didn't rush the process. Here was a courtesy passed from one waking soul to the next, something all the men sleeping in their coffins would one day rise to discover.

And eventually…forget.

# 1
2049 • Washington, D.C.

The tall glass trophy cabinets had once served as bookshelves. There were hints. Little things like hardware on the shelves that dated back centuries, while the hinges and the tiny locks went back mere decades. There was the clash of wood: the framing around the glass was cherry, but the cases had been built of oak. Someone had attempted to remedy this with a few coats of stain, but the grain didn't match. The color wasn't perfect. To trained eyes, details such as these were glaring.

Congressman Donald Keene gathered these clues without meaning to. He simply saw that long ago there had been a great purge, a making of space. At some point in the past, the Senator's waiting room had been stripped of its obligatory law books until only a handful of refugees remained. These beleaguered survivors, few in number, sat silently in the dim corners of the glass cabinets. They were shut-in, their spines laced with cracks, old leather flaking off like aged or sunburnt skin.

The rest of the books—all the survivors' kin—were gone. In their place stood a collection of mementos from the Senator's two lifetimes of service.

Reflected in the glass, Congressman Keene could see a handful of his fellow freshmen pacing and stirring, their terms of service newly begun. Like Donald, they were young and still hopelessly optimistic. They were bringing change to Capitol Hill. And this time, somehow, they hoped to deliver where their similarly naïve predecessors had not.

While they waited their turns to meet with the great Senator Thurman from their home state of Georgia, they chatted nervously amongst themselves. They were a gaggle of priests, Donald thought, all lined up to meet the Pope, to kiss his ring. He let out a heavy breath and focused on the contents of the case, lost himself in the treasures behind the glass while a fellow representative from Georgia prattled on about his district's Centers for Disease Control and Prevention.

"—and they have this detailed guide on their website, this response and readiness manual in case of, okay, get this, a zombie invasion! Can you believe that? Zombies. Like even the CDC thinks something could go wrong and suddenly we're all *eating* each other—"

Donald stifled a smile, fearful it would be spied in the glass. He looked over a collection of photographs, one each of the Senator with the last four presidents. It was the same pose and handshake in each shot, the same staged background of windless flags and fancy oversized seals. The Senator seemed hardly to change as the presidents came and went. His hair started white and it stayed white; he seemed perfectly unfazed by the passing of decades, as if this was how he'd always been.

Seeing the photographs side by side devalued each of them somehow. They looked staged. Phony. It was as if the world's most powerful men had begged their mommies to take their picture while they stood and posed with this cardboard cutout, this imposing plastic statue, some roadside attraction.

Donald laughed, and the congressman from Atlanta joined him.

"I know, right? Zombies. It's hilarious. But think about it, okay? Why would the CDC even *have* this field manual unless—?"

Donald wanted to correct his fellow freshman, to show him what he'd really been laughing about. Look at the smiles, he wanted to say. They were on the faces of the *presidents*. The Senator looked like he'd rather be anyplace else. It was as if each in this succession of commanders in chief knew who was the more powerful man, who would be there long after they had come and gone.

"—it's advice like, everyone should have a baseball bat with their flashlights and candles, right? Just in case. You know, for bashing brains."

Donald pulled out his phone and checked the time. He glanced at the door leading off the waiting room and wondered how much longer he'd have to wait. Putting the phone away, he studied a shelf where a military uniform had been carefully arranged like a delicate work of origami. The left breast of the jacket featured a Lego-brick wall of medals; the sleeves were folded over and pinned to highlight the gold braids sewn along the cuffs. In front of the uniform, a collection of decorative coins rested in a custom wooden rack, tokens of appreciation from the men and women still serving.

The two arrangements spoke volumes—this uniform from the past and these coins from those currently deployed. They were bookends on a pair of wars. One that the Senator had fought in as a youth. The other, a war he had battled to prevent as a grown and wiser man.

"—yeah, it sounds crazy, I know, but do you know what rabies does to a dog? I mean, what it *really* does, the biological—?"

Donald leaned close to his reflection and studied the decorative coins. The number and slogan on each one represented a deployed group. Or was it a battalion? He couldn't remember. His sister Charlotte would know. She was over there somewhere.

Before Donald could consider the long odds, he scanned a collection of framed photographs for her, a wall of pictures in the back of the glass cabinet featuring servicemen and servicewomen huddled around the Senator. He searched the faces among the sand-colored fatigues, all those smiles a long way from home.

"—you think the CDC knows something we don't? I mean, forget weaponized anthrax, imagine legions of *biters* breaking out all over the place—"

Most were Army photographs. And, of course, Charlotte wasn't in them. Donald studied one from the Navy. The Senator was standing on the deck of a ship with a crowd of men and women in neatly pressed uniforms. More smiles on warring faces. The ship may have been underway. The Senator's feet were planted wide, a breeze lifting his white hair, giving him a fierce mohawk—or maybe the comical tuft of a cockatiel. Above the group, stenciled in white paint on gunmetal gray: *USS The Sullivans*.

"Hey, aren't you even a little nervous about this?"

Donald realized he'd been asked a question. His focus drifted from the collection of photographs to the reflection of the chatty congressman in the glass. The man looked to be in his mid-thirties, probably Donald's age.

"Am I nervous about zombies?" He laughed. "No. Can't say that I am."

The congressman took a step closer, his eyes drifting toward the imposing uniform that stood propped up as if a warrior's chest remained inside. "No," the man said. "About meeting *him*."

The door to the reception area opened, bleeps from the phones on the other side leaking out.

"Congressman Keene?"

Donald turned away from one last display: a piece of shrapnel, a Purple Heart, a note from a wounded soldier expressing his undying thanks. An elderly receptionist stood in the doorway, her white blouse and black skirt highlighting a thin and athletic frame.

"Senator Thurman will see you now," she said.

Donald patted the congressman from Atlanta on the shoulder as he stepped past.

"Hey, good luck," the gentleman stammered after him.

Donald smiled. He fought the temptation to turn and tell the man that he knew the Senator well enough, that he had been bounced on his knee back when he was but a child. Only—Donald was too busy concealing his own nerves to bother. This was different. He stepped through the deeply paneled door of rich hardwoods and entered the Senator's noisy inner sanctum. This wasn't like passing through a foyer to pick up a man's daughter for a date. This was the pressure of meeting as colleagues when Donald still felt like that same toddler from his bronco-knee days.

"Through here," the receptionist said. She guided Donald between pairs of wide and busy desks, a dozen phones chirping in short bursts that sounded more medical than senatorial. Young men and women in suits and crisp blouses double-fisted receivers while somehow remaining calm. Their bored expressions suggested that this was a normal workload for a weekday morning. It wasn't as if the world was coming to an end, or anything.

Donald reached out a hand as he passed one of the desks, brushing the wood with his fingertips. Mahogany. The aides here had desks nicer than his own. And the decor: the plush carpet, the broad and ancient crown molding, the antique tile ceiling, the dangling light fixtures that may have been actual crystal. Everything was noticeably more opulent in the Dirksen Senate building. It was the House of Lords compared to Rayburn across the street, Donald's own House of Commons.

At the end of the buzzing and bleeping room, a paneled door opened and disgorged Congressman Mick Webb, just finished with his meeting. Mick didn't notice Donald, was too absorbed by the open manila folder he held in front of him.

Donald stopped and waited for his colleague and old college acquaintance to approach. "So," he asked Mick. "How did it go?"

Mick looked up and snapped the folder shut. He tucked it under his arm and nodded. "Yeah, yeah. It went great." He smiled. "Sorry if we ran long. The old man couldn't get enough of me."

Donald laughed. "No problem." He jabbed a thumb over his shoulder. "I was making new friends."

Mick smiled. "I bet."

"Yeah, well, I'll see you back at Rayburn."

"Sure thing." Mick slapped him on the arm with the folder and headed for the exit. Donald caught the impatient glare from the Senator's receptionist and hurried over. She waved him through the old door and into the dimly lit office before shutting it tight against the bleeping phones.

"Congressman Keene."

Senator Paul Thurman stood from behind his desk and stretched out a hand. He flashed a familiar smile, one Donald had come to recognize as much from photos and TV as from his childhood. Despite Thurman's age—he had to be pushing seventy if he wasn't already there—the Senator was trim and fit. His oxford shirt hugged a military frame; a thick neck bulged out of his knotted tie; his white hair remained as crisp and orderly as an enlisted man's.

Donald crossed the dark room and accepted the hand that had clasped that of so many presidents.

"Good to see you, sir."

As his fist was pumped up and down, he imagined flash bulbs popping and expensive cameras clicking wildly. He almost turned to the side and adopted a frozen and smiling pose, thinking the Senator would get the joke at once. Fortunately, the urge passed. Donald reminded himself that he wasn't there to date the Senator's daughter but to serve alongside him.

"Please, sit." Thurman released Donald's hand and gestured to one of the chairs across from his desk. Donald turned and lowered himself into the bright red leather, the gold grommets along the arm like sturdy rivets in a steel beam.

"How's Helen?"

"Helen?" Donald straightened his tie. "She's great. She's back in Savannah. She really enjoyed seeing you at the reception."

"She's a beautiful woman, your wife."

"Thank you, sir." Donald fought to relax, which didn't help. The office had the pall of dusk, even with the overhead lights on. The clouds outside had turned nasty—low and dark. If it rained, he would have to take the tunnel back to his office. He hated the tunnel. They could carpet it and hang those little chandeliers at intervals, but he could still tell he was below ground. The tunnels in Washington made him feel like a rat scurrying through a sewer. It always seemed like the roof was about to cave in.

"How's the job treating you so far?"

Donald shifted his gaze away from the clouds. "The job's good," he said. "It's busy, but good."

He started to ask the Senator how Anna was doing, but the door behind him opened before he could. The discordant cries of the busy phones disturbed the quiet as the thin receptionist entered and delivered two bottles of water. Donald thanked her, twisted the cap off, and saw that it had been pre-opened. Just like at that fancy steakhouse the lobbyist from the PAGW had taken him to.

"I hope you're not too busy to work on something for me." Senator Thurman raised an eyebrow. Donald took a sip of water and wondered if that was a skill one could master, that eyebrow lift. It was effective as hell. It made him want to jump to attention and salute.

"Oh, I can make the time," he said. "After all the stumping you did for me? I doubt I would've made it past the primaries." He held the water bottle in his lap. When he crossed his legs, he became aware of his brown socks and black pants. He lowered his foot back to the ground and wished Helen had stayed in D.C. longer.

"You and Mick Webb go back, right? Both Bulldogs."

It took Donald a moment to realize the Senator was referring to their college mascot. He hadn't spent a lot of time at Georgia following sports. "Yessir. Go Dawgs."

He hoped that was right.

The Senator smiled. He leaned forward so that his face caught the soft light raining down on his desk. Donald watched as shadows caught in wrinkles otherwise easy to miss. Thurman's lean face and square chin made him look younger straight-on than he probably did from the side. Here was a man who got places by approaching others directly rather than in ambush.

"You studied architecture at Georgia."

Donald nodded. It was easy to forget that he knew Thurman better than the Senator knew him. One of them grabbed far more newspaper headlines than the other.

"That's right. For my undergrad. I went into planning for my master's. I figured I could do more good governing people than I could drawing boxes to put them in."

He winced to hear himself deliver the line. It was a pat phrase from grad school, something he should've left behind with crushing beer cans on his forehead and ogling asses in skirts. He wondered for the dozenth time why he and the other congressional newcomers had been summoned. When he first got the invite, he figured it was a social visit. Then Mick bragged about his own appointment, and Donald figured it was some kind of formality or tradition. But now he wondered if this was a power play, a chance to butter up the Reps from Georgia for those times when Thurman would need a particular vote in the lower and *lesser* house.

"Tell me, Donny—" The Senator reached for his bottle of water, glanced up. "How good are you at keeping secrets?"

Donald's blood ran cold. He forced himself to laugh off the sudden flush of nerves.

"I got elected, didn't I?"

Senator Thurman smiled. "And so you probably learned the best lesson there is about secrets." He raised his plastic bottle in salute. "*Denial.*"

Donald nodded and took a sip of his own water. He wasn't sure where this was going, but he already felt uneasy. He sensed some of the backroom dealings coming on that he'd promised his constituents he'd root out if elected.

The Senator leaned back in his chair.

"Denial is the secret sauce in this town," he said. "It's the flavor that holds all the other ingredients together. Here's what I tell the newly elected: the truth is gonna get out—it always does—but it's gonna blend in with all the *lies*." The Senator twirled a hand in the air. "You have to deny each lie and every truth with the same vinegar. Let those websites and blowhards who bitch about cover-ups confuse the public *for* you."

"Uh, yessir." Donald didn't know what else to say. This seemed like a strange conversation to be having. He took another gulp of water.

The Senator lifted an eyebrow again. He remained frozen for a pause, and then asked, out of nowhere: "Do you believe in aliens, Donny?"

Donald nearly lost the water out of his nose. He covered his mouth with his hand, coughed, had to wipe his chin. The Senator didn't budge.

"Aliens?" Donald shook his head and wiped his wet palm on his thigh. "Nossir. I mean, not the abducting kind. Why?"

He wondered if this was some kind of debriefing. Why had the Senator asked him if he could keep a secret? Was this a security initiation? The Senator remained silent.

"They're not real," Donald finally said. He watched for any twitch or hint. "Are they?"

The old man cracked a smile. "That's the thing," he said. "If they are or they aren't, the chatter out there would be the exact same. Would you be surprised if I told you they're very much real?"

"Hell, yeah, I'd be surprised."

"Good." The Senator slid a folder across the desk. Donald eyed it and held up a hand.

"Wait. Are they real or aren't they? What're you trying to tell me?"

Senator Thurman laughed. "Of course they're not real. Are you kidding?" He took his hand off the folder and propped his elbows on the desk. "Have you seen how much NASA wants from us so they can fly to Mars and back? No way we're getting to another star. Ever. And no one's coming here. Hell, why would they?"

Donald didn't know *what* to think, which was a far cry from how he'd felt less than a minute ago. He saw what the Senator meant, how truth and lies seemed black and white, but mixed together, they made everything gray and confusing. He glanced down at the folder. It looked similar to the one Mick had been carrying and reminded him of the government's fondness for all things outdated.

"This is denial, right?" He studied the Senator. "That's what you're doing right now. You're trying to throw me off."

"No. This is me telling you to stop watching so many science fiction flicks. In fact, why is it you think those eggheads are always dreaming of colonizing some other planet? You have any idea what would be involved? It's ludicrous. Not cost effective."

Donald shrugged. He didn't think it was ludicrous. He twisted the cap back onto his water. "It's in our nature to dream of open space," he said. "To find room to spread out in. Isn't that how we ended up here?"

"Here? In America?" The Senator laughed. "We didn't come here and find open space. We got a bunch of people sick, killed them, and *made* space." Thurman pointed at the folder. "Which brings me to this. I've got something I'd like you to work on."

Donald leaned forward and placed his bottle on the leather inlay of the formidable desk. He took the folder.

"Is this something coming through committee?"

He tried to temper his hopes. It was alluring to think of

co-authoring a bill his first year in office. He opened the folder and tilted it toward the window where storms were gathering.

"No, nothing like that. This is about CAD-FAC."

Donald nodded. *Of course.* The preamble about secrets and conspiracies suddenly made perfect sense, as did the gathering of Georgia congressmen outside. This was about the Containment and Disposal Facility at the heart of the Senator's new energy bill, the complex that would one day house most of the world's spent nuclear fuel. Or, according to the websites Thurman had alluded to, it was going to be the next Area 51, or the site where a new-and-improved superbomb was being built, or a place where mad scientists would tunnel to the center of the Earth to prevent the core from melting down, or a secure holding facility for Libertarians who had purchased one too many guns at Walmart. Take your pick. There was enough noise out there to hide *any* truth.

"Yeah," Donald said, deflated. "I've been getting some entertaining calls from my district." He didn't dare mention the one about the Lizard People, or the one that had to do with magnetic poles flipping. "I want you to know, sir, that privately I'm behind the facility one hundred percent." He looked up at the Senator. "I'm glad I didn't have to vote on it publicly, of course, but it was about time *someone* offered up their backyard, right?"

"Precisely. For the common good." Senator Thurman took a long pull from his water, and Donald noticed for the first time that his office didn't reek of old cigar smoke, wasn't infused with the stench of pipe tobacco, aged leather, expensive whiskey, and the other deal-making scents he constantly nosed back at Rayburn. Hell, despite Helen's aromatic electric candles, his own office still stank like the eight-term Representative he'd ousted in the primaries—the one who *had* voted on the energy bill.

Thurman leaned back in his chair and cleared his throat. "You're a sharp young man, Donny. Not everyone sees what a boon to our state this'll be. A real life-saver." He smiled. "I'm sorry, you *are* still going by Donny, right? Or is it Donald, now?"

"Either's fine," Donald lied. He no longer enjoyed being called Donny, but changing names in the middle of one's life was practically impossible. He returned to the folder and flipped the cover letter over. There was a drawing underneath, a drawing that struck him as being out of place. It was...too familiar. Familiar, and yet it didn't belong there—it was from another life. It was as if he'd woken up and found in his bed some object he'd clutched in a dream.

"Have you seen the economic reports?" Thurman asked. "Do you know how many jobs this bill created overnight?" He snapped his fingers. "Forty thousand, just like that. And that's just from Georgia. A lot will be from your district, a lot of shipping, a lot of stevedores. Of course, now that it's passed, our less nimble colleagues are grumbling that *they* should've had a chance to bid—"

"I drew this," Donald interrupted, pulling out the sheet of paper. He showed it to Thurman as if the Senator would be surprised to see it had snuck into the folder. Donald wondered if this was the Senator's daughter's doing, some kind of a joke or *hello-and-wink* from Anna.

Thurman nodded. "Yes, well, it needs more detail, wouldn't you say?"

Donald studied the architectural illustration and wondered what sort of test this was. He remembered the drawing. It was a last-minute project for his biotecture class his senior year. There was nothing unusual or amazing about it. His professor had given him a B, the red ink still tinged purple from where it had bled into the overlapping streaks of blue sky.

With an impartial eye, Donald would give the project a C+. It was spare where his classmates had been bold, utilitarian where he could've taken risks. Green tufts jutted up from the flat roof, a horrible cliché. Half the building was cut away to reveal the interspersed levels for housing, working, and shopping.

In sum, it was drab and boring. Donald couldn't imagine a design so bare rising from the deserts of Dubai alongside the great new breed of self-sustaining skyscrapers. He certainly couldn't see what the Senator wanted him to do with it, other than maybe burn it to the ground.

"More detail," he murmured, repeating the Senator's words. He flipped through the rest of the folder, looking for hints, for context.

"Hm." Thurman sipped from his water bottle.

"Wait." Donald studied a list of requirements written up as if by a prospective client. "This looks like a design proposal." Words he had forgotten he'd ever learned caught his eye: interior traffic flow, block plan, HVAC, hydroponics—

"You'll have to lose the sunlight." Senator Thurman's chair squeaked as he leaned over his desk. He moved Donald's sweating bottle to a coaster and wiped the leather dry with his palm.

"I'm sorry?"

"It's nothing. Forget about it." Thurman waved his hand, obviously meaning the circle of moisture left by Donald's bottle.

"No, you said sunlight." Donald held the folder up. "What exactly are you wanting me to do?"

"I would suggest those lights like my wife uses." He cupped his hand into a tiny circle and pointed at the center. "She gets these tiny seeds to sprout in the winter, uses bulbs that cost me a goddamned fortune."

"You mean grow lights."

Thurman snapped his fingers. "And don't worry about the cost. Whatever you need. I'm also going to get you some help with the mechanical stuff. An engineer. An entire team."

Donald flipped through more of the folder. "What is this *for*? And why me?"

"This is what we call a *just-in-case* building. Probably'll never get used, but they won't let us store the fuel rods out there unless we put this bugger nearby. It's like this window in my basement I had to lower before our house could pass inspection. It was for...what do you call it—?"

"Egress," Donald said, the word flowing back unaided.

Thurman snapped his fingers. "Right. Egress." He pointed to the folder. "This building is like that window, something we've gotta build so the rest'll pass inspection. This'll be where—in the unlikely event of an attack or a leak—where facility employees can go. You know, like a shelter. And it needs to be *perfect* or this project'll be shut down faster than a tick's wink. Just because our bill passed and got signed doesn't mean we're home free, Donny. There was that project out west that got okayed decades ago, scored funding. Eventually, it fell through."

Donald knew the one he was talking about. A containment facility buried under a mountain. The buzz on the Hill was that the Georgia project had the same chances of success. The folder suddenly tripled in weight as he considered this. He was being asked to be a part of this future failure. He would be staking his newly won office on it.

"I've got Mick Webb working on something related. Logistics and planning, really. You two will need to collaborate on a few things. And Anna is taking leave from her post at MIT to lend a hand."

"*Anna?*" Donald fumbled for his water, his hand shaking.

"Of course. She'll be your lead engineer on this project. There are details in there on what she'll need, space-wise."

Donald took a gulp of water and forced himself to swallow.

"There's a lot of other people I could call in, sure, but this project can't fail, you understand? It needs to be like *family*. People I can trust." Senator Thurman interlocked his fingers. "If this is the only thing you were elected to do, I want you to do it right. It's why I stumped for you in the first place."

"Of course." Donald bobbed his head to hide his confusion. He had worried during the election that the Senator's endorsement stemmed from old family ties. This was somehow worse. Donald hadn't been using the Senator at all; it was the *other way around*. Studying the drawing in his lap, the newly elected congressman felt one job he was inadequately trained for melt away—only to be replaced by a *different* job that seemed equally daunting.

"Wait," he said. "I still don't get it." He studied the old drawing. "Why the grow lights?"

Senator Thurman reached for his bottle and polished off his water, the empty plastic crinkling in his fist. He smacked his lips and turned to toss the bottle into a blue recycling bin. And his profile, Donald saw, was every bit as chiseled and handsome as the face he presented to the cameras. He had barely changed in all the years Donald had known him.

"Because, Donny—" He turned and smiled. "This building I want you to design for me—it's going to go *below* ground."

# 2
2110 • Silo 1

Troy held his breath and tried to remain calm while the doctor pumped the rubber bulb. The inflatable band swelled around his bicep until it pinched his skin. He wasn't sure if slowing his breathing and steadying his pulse affected his blood pressure, but he had a strong urge to impress the man in the white coveralls. He wanted his numbers to come back *normal*.

His arm throbbed a few beats while the needle bounced and the air hissed out.

"Eighty over fifty." The band made a ripping sound as it was torn loose. Troy rubbed the spot where his skin had been pinched.

"Is that okay?"

The doctor made a note on his clipboard. "It's low, but not outside the norm." Behind him, his assistant labeled a cup of dark gray urine before placing it inside a small fridge. Troy caught sight of a half-eaten sandwich among the samples, not even wrapped.

He looked down at his bare knees sticking out of the blue paper gown. His legs were pale and seemed smaller than he remembered. Bony. He felt the urge to pee but had already gone as much as he could.

"I still can't make a fist," he told the doctor, working his fingers in and out.

"That's perfectly normal. Your strength will return. Look into the light, please."

Troy followed the bright beam and tried not to blink.

"How long have you been doing this?" he asked the doctor.

"You're my third coming out. I've put two under." He lowered the light and smiled at Troy. "I've only been out myself for less than a month. I can tell you that the strength will return."

Troy nodded. The doctor's assistant came over and handed him another pill and a cup of water. Troy hesitated a moment. He stared down at the little blue capsule nestled in the crease of his life line.

"A double dose this morning," the doctor said, "and then you'll be given one with breakfast and dinner. Please do not skip a treatment."

Troy looked up. "What happens if I don't take it?"

The doctor shook his head and frowned. He didn't say.

Troy popped the pill in his mouth and chased it with the water. The cup looked identical to the one he'd peed in. He hoped they washed them thoroughly. A bitterness slid down his throat.

"One of my assistants will bring you some clothes and a fluid meal to kick-start your gut. If you have any dizziness or chills, you're to call me at once. Otherwise, we'll see you back here in six months." The doctor made a note, then chuckled. "Well, someone else will see you. My shift will be over."

"Okay." Troy shivered. The doctor looked up from his clipboard.

"You're not cold, are you? I keep it a little extra warm in here."

Troy hesitated before answering. "No, doctor. I'm not cold. Not anymore."

••••

Troy entered the lift at the end of the hall, his legs still weak, and studied the array of numbered buttons. The orders they'd given him included directions to his office, but he vaguely remembered how to get there. Much of his orientation had survived the decades of sleep; it was other items that seemed to be slipping away.

Memory wasn't supposed to work like this. He felt as though he were on a ship beset by fog. There were breaks where he could spot the shoreline, the recent past, but much of what lay inland was obscured. And there were voices ringing there and carrying out over the water. Troy sensed bad things happening to the people deep in the woods.

The doors to the lift closed automatically, and he shook away the image. His apartment was on thirty-seven; he remembered that. His office was on thirty-four. He reached for a button, intending to head straight to his desk, and instead found his hand sliding up to the very top. He still had a few minutes before he needed to be anywhere, and he felt some strange urge, some tug, to get as high as possible, to rise through the soil pressing in from all sides.

The button for the top floor clicked and glowed to life as he applied pressure. Something loomed above him. He could feel an attraction upward, a thread running clear through the top of his skull and yanking him like a puppet. There was something there he needed to see, something he'd left behind.

Troy struggled to remember as the lift lurched upward. He groped for this gossamer and fading dream, this glimpse through the mist—but the bitterness in his throat and the pills in his stomach were a tide tugging him away from the shore. Why had he been crying earlier? Or had he cried? He couldn't remember. His stomach grumbled around the shake he'd been forced to drink. He shivered but was not cold.

The elevator accelerated up the shaft. There was a whooshing sound as another car or maybe the counterweight zoomed by. He knew these things. The round buttons flashed as the floors passed. There was an enormous spread of them, seventy in all. The centers of many were dull from years of rubbing. This didn't seem right. Just yesterday, the buttons were shiny and new. Just yesterday, *everything* was.

Gravity weakened as the elevator slowed, and Troy palmed the wall for balance, his legs still uncertain.

The door dinged and slid open. Troy blinked at the bright lights in the hallway. He left the elevator and followed a short walk toward a room leaking chatter. His new boots were stiff on his feet, the generic gray coveralls itchy. He tried to imagine four more times of waking up like this, feeling this weak and disoriented. Five shifts of six months each. Five shifts he hadn't volunteered for. He wondered if it would get progressively easier or if it would only get worse.

The bustle in the cafeteria seemed to modulate as he entered. A few heads turned his way, utensils pausing. He saw at once that his gray coveralls weren't so generic. There was a scattering of colors seated at the tables, forks paused between plate and mouth. A large cluster of reds, quite a few yellows. No other grays.

That first meal of sticky paste he'd been given rumbled once more in his stomach. He wasn't allowed to eat anything else for six hours, which made the aroma from the canned foods overwhelming. He remembered the fare, had lived on it during his orientation. His orientation after—

He couldn't remember. It was there, but he was losing it. And the food he had once grown tired of suddenly seemed appetizing.

"Sir."

A young man nodded to Troy as he walked past, angling for the elevators. Troy thought he recognized the man, couldn't be sure. Dreams intervened. The gentleman certainly seemed to have recognized *him*. Or was it the gray coveralls that stood out?

"First shift?"

An older gentleman approached, thin, with white and wispy hair that circled his head from temple to temple. He held a tray in his hands, smiled at Troy. Pulling open a recycling bin, he slid the entire tray inside and dropped it with a clatter.

"Come up for the view?" the man asked.

Troy nodded. It was all men throughout the cafeteria. All men. They had explained why this was safer. He tried to remember as the man with the splotches of age on his skin crossed his arms and stood beside him. There were no introductions. Troy wondered if names meant less amid the short shifts and long dreams. He gazed out over the bustling tables toward the massive screen that covered the far wall.

Here was the shoreline and the edge of the wood—some part of the thing that was wrong. And sure enough, a real mist roamed the view, whirls of dust and hanging clouds over a field of scattered and half-eaten debris. A few metal poles bristled from the ground and sagged lifeless, the tents and flags long vanished. Troy remembered. He couldn't name it, but his stomach twisted in recognition; it tightened like a fist around the paste and the bitter pill.

"This'll be my second shift," the man said.

Troy barely heard. His watering eyes drifted across the lifeless hills, the gray slopes rising up toward dark clouds full of menacing and invisible things. The debris scattered everywhere was rotting away, molecules taking flight. Next shift, or the one after, it would all be gone.

"You can see further from the lounge." The man turned and gestured along the wall. Troy knew well enough what room he was referring to. This part of the building was familiar to him in ways this man could hardly guess.

"No, but thanks," he stammered. Troy waved him off. "I think I've seen enough."

Curious faces returned to their trays; the chatter resumed. It was sprinkled with the clinking of spoons and forks on metal bowls and plates. Troy turned and left without saying another word. He put that hideous view behind him—turned his back on the unspoken eeriness of it. He hurried, shivering, toward the elevator, knees weak with more than the long rest. He needed to be alone, didn't want anyone around him this time, didn't want sympathetic hands comforting him while he cried.

# 3
2049 • Washington, D.C.

Donald kept the thick folder tucked inside his jacket and hurried through the rain. He had chosen to get soaked crossing the square rather than face his claustrophobia in the tunnels.

Traffic hissed by on the wet asphalt. He waited for a gap, ignored the crosswalk signals, and scooted across.

Rayburn's marble steps gleamed treacherously wet. A woman in a black dress clopped up them in heels, an umbrella held low, and Donald wondered how this mad dash of his made more sense than the carpeted hallway beneath the streets. By avoiding an irrational fear, he was putting himself in real danger. Slick steps and cutting through traffic—the banal claimed far more than the subject of strange phobias.

A doorman in a red jacket stood on the portico, out of the rain. He reached for the long brass handle, grabbed a dark patch of patina, and pulled the door open for the woman in the heels. She shook the rain loose from her umbrella, brushed her hair, and ducked inside. Donald thanked the doorman and followed. He caught a glimpse of his matted and dripping hair in the glass.

Inside, a Security officer stood impassively while badges were scanned, red unblinking eyes beeping at barcodes. The woman spun through the turnstile, and then Donald. He checked the folder Thurman had given him, made sure it was still dry, and wondered why such archaic things were considered safer than an email or a digital copy.

His office was one floor up. He headed for the stairs, preferring them to Rayburn's ancient and slow lift. His shoes squeaked on the tile as he left the plush runner by the door.

The hallway upstairs was its usual mess. Two high schoolers from the page program hurried past, most likely fetching coffee. A TV crew stood outside of Amanda Kelly's office, the lights on the camera bathing her and a young reporter in a daytime glow. Concerned voters and eager lobbyists were identifiable by the guest passes hanging around their necks. They were easy to distinguish from one another, these two groups. The voters wore frowns and invariably seemed lost. The lobbyists were the ones with the Cheshire grins who navigated the halls more confidently than even the newly elected.

Donald opened the folder and pretended to read as he made his way through the chaos, hoping to avoid conversation. He squeezed behind the cameraman and ducked into his office next door.

"Mr. Keene."

Margaret, his secretary, stood up from her desk. She grabbed a pack of mail and held it out, a handful of notes stuck to the top.

Donald took the envelopes and piled them onto his folder. Margaret lowered her voice.

"Sir, you have a *visitor*."

Donald glanced around the waiting room. It was empty. He saw that the door to his office was partway open.

"I'm sorry I let her in." Margaret mimed carrying a box, her hands at her waist and her back arched. "She had a delivery. Said it was from the Senator."

Donald waved her concerns aside. Margaret was older than him, in her mid-forties, and had come highly recommended, but she did have a conspiratorial streak. Perhaps it came with the years of experience.

"It's fine," Donald assured her. He found it interesting that there were a hundred senators, two from his state, but only one was referred to as *the Senator*. "I'll see what it's about. In the meantime, I need you to free up a daily block in my schedule. An hour or two in the morning would be ideal." He flashed her the folder. "I've got something that's going to eat up quite a bit of time."

Margaret nodded and sat down in front of her computer. Donald turned toward his office.

"Oh, sir—?"

He looked back. She pointed to her own head. "Your *hair*," she hissed.

He patted his head and remembered the glimpse he'd caught earlier. He ran his fingers through hair matted down by the rain, and drops of water leapt off him like startled fleas. Margaret frowned and lifted her shoulders in a helpless shrug. Donald gave up and pushed his office door open, expecting to find someone sitting in one of the chairs across from his desk.

Instead, he saw someone wiggling *underneath* it.

"Hello?"

The door bumped into something on the floor. Donald peeked around and saw a large box with a picture of a computer monitor on it. He glanced at the desk, saw the display was already set up.

"Oh, hey!"

The greeting was muffled by the hollow beneath his desk. Slender hips in a herringbone skirt wiggled back toward him. Donald knew who it was before her head emerged. He felt a flush of guilt, of anger at her being there unannounced.

"You know, you should have your cleaning lady dust under here once in a while." Anna Thurman stood and smiled. She slapped her palms together, brushing them off before extending one his way. Donald shifted the folder and envelopes; he dropped a few of the latter as he fumbled to shake her hand.

"Hey, stranger."

"Yeah. Hey." He bent to retrieve the mail, losing a few more pieces in the process. Rain dribbled down his cheek and neck, hiding any sudden flush of perspiration. "What's going on?" He stood and dumped the mail on his desk, walked around it to create some space between them—some room so he could breathe. The monitor sat there looking at him innocently, a film of protective plastic blurring the screen.

"Dad thought you might need an extra one." Anna tucked a loose clump of auburn hair behind her ear. She still possessed the same alluring and elfin quality when they poked out like that. "I volunteered," she explained, shrugging.

"Oh." He placed the folder on his desk and thought about the drawing of the building he had briefly suspected was from her. And now, here she was. Checking his reflection in the new monitor, he saw the mess he had made of his hair. He reached up and tried to smooth it.

"Another thing," Anna said. "Your computer would be better off *on* your desk. I know it's unsightly, but the dust is gonna choke that thing to death. Dust is *murder* on these guys."

"Yeah. Okay."

He sat down and realized he could no longer see the chair across from his desk. He slid the new monitor to one side while Anna walked around and stood beside him, her arms crossed, completely relaxed in his presence. As if they'd seen each other yesterday and all the days before.

"I think you'll want one more." She pointed to the other side of his original monitor. She wasn't standing there to make him uncomfortable—she'd been surveying his workspace. "I can bring a splitter and set it up for you. Maybe untangle those wires while I'm at it."

"Oh. Okay."

He halfway expected her to tousle his hair while she patronized him. He physically flinched at the thought. Just conjuring the image made it feel as though it were bound to happen—or already had. He rolled his chair away and made a show of adjusting the other monitor.

"So," he said. "You're in town."

"Since last week. I was gonna stop by and see you and Helen on Saturday, but I've been so busy getting settled into my apartment. Unboxing things, you know?"

"Yeah." He accidentally bumped the mouse, and the old monitor winked on. His computer was running. The terror of being in the same room with an ex subsided just enough for the timing of the day's events to dawn on him.

"Wait." He turned to Anna. "So you were over here *installing* this while your father was asking me if I was interested in his project?"

She raised an eyebrow. Donald realized it wasn't something one learned—it was a talent her clan passed from parent to child.

"He practically gift-wrapped the election for you," she said flatly.

Donald reached for the folder and riffed the pages like a deck of cards. "You know," he said, "the *illusion* of free will would've been nice. That's all."

Anna laughed. She was about to tousle his hair, he could feel it. Dropping his hand from the folder and patting his jacket pocket, he felt for his phone. It was like Helen was there with him. He felt the urge to call her.

"Was Dad at least gentle with you?"

He looked up to see that she hadn't moved. Her arms were still crossed, his hair untousled, nothing to panic about.

"What? Oh, yeah. Your father was fine. Like old times. In fact, it's like he hasn't aged a day."

Smiling, she picked up something from his desk. A twist tie. From the monitor's cord, perhaps. "He doesn't really age, you know." She crossed the room and picked up large molded pieces of foam and slid them noisily into the empty box. Donald found his eyes drifting toward her skirt and forced himself to look away.

"He takes nano treatments almost religiously. Started

because of his knees. The military covered it for a while. Now he swears by them."

"I didn't know that," Donald lied. He'd heard rumors, of course. It was "Botox for the whole body," people said. Better than testosterone supplements. It cost a fortune, and you wouldn't live forever, but you could sure as hell delay the pain of aging. He'd read a story recently about a guy who had died in the middle of a triathlon. A hundred-and-ten years old. His grandkids didn't sound upset at all, said he was doing what he loved right up to the end.

Anna narrowed her eyes. "You don't think there's anything *wrong* with that, do you?"

"What? No. It's fine, I guess. I just wouldn't. Wait, why? Don't tell me you've been—?"

Anna rested her hands on her hips and cocked her head to the side. There was something oddly seductive about the defensive posture, something that whisked away the years since he'd last seen her.

"Do you think I would *need* to?" she asked him.

"No, no. It's not that—" He waved his hands. "It's just that *I* don't think I ever would."

A smirk thinned her lips. Maturity had hardened Anna's good looks, had refined her lean frame, but the fierceness from her youth remained. "You say that now," she said, "but wait until your joints start to ache and your back goes out from something as simple as turning your head too fast. Then you'll see."

"Okay. Well." He clapped his hands together. "This has been quite the day for catching up on old times." Peeking again at the shiny new monitor, he gave his hair another minor adjustment.

"Yes, it has. Now, what day works best for you?" Anna interlocked the flaps on the large box and slid it toward the door with her foot. She walked around the back of the desk and stood beside him, a hand on his chair, the other reaching for his mouse.

"What *day*—?"

He watched while she changed some settings on his computer and the new monitor flashed to life. Donald could feel his pulse in his crotch, could smell a familiar perfume. The breeze she had caused by walking across the room seemed to stir all around him. Her body had pressed against air molecules that now pressed into him. This felt near enough to a caress, to a physical touch, that he wondered if he was cheating on Helen right at that very moment while Anna did little more than adjust sliders on his control panel.

"You know how to use this, right?" She slid the mouse from one screen to the other, dragging an old game of solitaire with it.

"Uh, yeah." Donald squirmed in his seat. "Um...what do you mean about a day that works best for me?"

She let go of the mouse. It felt like she had taken her hand off his thigh. Stepping away from him, she peeled the plastic film off the monitor with a loud ripping sound and balled it up in her hands.

"Dad wants me to handle the mechanical spaces on the plans." She gestured toward the folder as if she knew precisely what was inside. "I'm taking a sabbatical from the Institute until this Atlanta project is up and running. I thought we'd want to meet once a week to go over things."

"Oh. Well. I'll have to get back with you on that. My schedule here is crazy. It's different every day."

He imagined what Helen would say to he and Anna getting together once a week.

"We could, you know, set up a shared space in AutoCAD," he suggested. "I can link you into my document—"

She nodded. "We could do that."

"And email back and forth. Or video chat. You know?"

Anna frowned. Donald realized he was being too obvious. She scrunched the ball of plastic film in her hand, the material squeaking in complaint. "Yeah, let's set up something like that," she said.

There was a flash of disappointment on her face as she turned for the box, and Donald felt the urge to apologize, but doing so would spell out the problem in neon lights: *I don't trust myself around you. We're not going to be friends. What the fuck are you doing here?*

"You really need to do something about the dust." She glanced back at his desk. "Seriously, your computer is going to choke on it."

"Okay. I will." He stood and hurried around his desk to walk her out. Anna stooped for the box.

"I can get that."

"Don't be silly." She stood with the large box pinned between one arm and her hip. She smiled and tucked her hair behind her ear. She could've been leaving his dorm room in college. There was that same awkward moment of a morning goodbye in last night's clothes.

"Okay, so you have my email?" he asked.

"You're in the blue pages now," she reminded him.

"Yeah."

"You look great, by the way." And before he could flinch back or defend himself, she was fixing his hair, her eyes lifting up, a smile on her lips.

Donald froze. His brain shut down completely.

When it came back online some time later, Anna was gone, leaving him standing there alone, soaked in guilt.

# 4
2110 • Silo 1

Troy was going to be late. The first day of his first shift, already a blubbering mess, and he was going to be late. In his rush to get away from the cafeteria, to be alone, he had taken the non-express by accident. Now, as he tried to compose himself and stop his nose from running, the lift seemed intent on stopping at every floor on the way down to load and unload passengers.

He stood in the corner as the lift stopped again and checked to see how bloodshot his eyes were in the elevator's silvery wall. A man wrestled a cart full of heavy boxes onto the lift. A gentleman with a load of green onions crowded inside behind him and stood close to Troy for a few stops. Nobody spoke. When the man with the onions got off, the smell remained. Troy shivered, one violent quake that traveled up his back and into his arms, but he thought nothing of it. He got off on thirty-four and tried to remember why he had been upset earlier.

The central elevator shaft emptied onto a narrow hallway on thirty-four. The hallway funneled him into a security station. The floor plan was vaguely familiar and yet somehow alien. It was unnerving to note the signs of wear in the carpet and the patch of dull steel in the middle of the turnstile where thighs had rubbed against it over the years. These were years that didn't exist for Troy. This wear and tear had shown up as if by magic.

The lone guard on duty looked up from something he was reading and nodded in greeting. Troy placed his palm on a screen that had grown hazy from use. There was no chit-chat, no small talk, no expectation of forming a lasting relationship. The light above the console flashed green, there was a loud click from the pedestal, and a little more sheen was rubbed off the revolving bar as Troy pushed through.

The guard smiled at him before returning his attention to his small tablet, probably some smut or a detective novel. At the end of the hallway, Troy paused and pulled his orders out of his breast pocket. There was a note on the back from the doctor. He flipped it over and turned the little map around to face the right direction, was pretty sure he knew the way, but everything was going in and out of focus.

The red dash marks on the map reminded him of fire safety plans he'd seen on walls somewhere else. Following the route took him past a string of small offices. Clacking keyboards, people talking, phones ringing—the sounds of everyday work made him feel suddenly tired. It also ignited a burn of insecurity, of having taken on something far larger than himself, a job he surely couldn't perform.

"Troy?"

He stopped and looked back at the man standing in the doorway he had just passed. A glance at his map and a twinge of recollection showed him he'd almost missed his office.

"That's me."

"Merriman." The gentleman didn't offer his hand. "You're late. Step inside."

Merriman turned and disappeared into the office. Troy followed, his legs sore from so much walking. He recognized the man, or thought he did. Couldn't remember if it was from the orientation or somewhen else. The dreams faded with each moment he was awake. It was like those nightmares that washed away in the morning shower, spiraling down and out of reach.

"Sorry I'm late," Troy started to explain, "I got on the wrong elevator—"

Merriman raised a hand. "That's fine. Do you need a drink?"

"They fed me."

"Of course." Merriman grabbed a thermos off his desk, the contents a bright blue. Troy remembered the foul taste. His tongue flinched as if he were suffering the same swig that Merriman took. The older man smacked his lips and let out a breath as he lowered the thermos.

"That stuff's awful," he said.

"Yeah." Troy looked around the office, his post for the next six months. The place, he figured, had aged quite a bit. Merriman, too. If he was a little grayer from the past six months, it was hard to tell, but he had kept the place in order. Troy resolved to extend the same courtesy to the next guy.

"You remember your briefing?" Merriman shuffled some folders on his desk.

"Like it was yesterday."

Merriman glanced up, a smirk on his face. "Right. Well, there hasn't been anything exciting the last few months. We had some mechanical issues when I started my shift but worked through those. There's a guy named Jones you'll want to use. He's been out a few weeks and is a lot sharper than the last guy. Been a lifesaver for me. He works down on sixty-eight with the power plant, but he's good just about anywhere, can fix pretty much anything."

Troy nodded. "Jones. Got it."

"Okay. Well, I left you some notes in these folders. There's been a few workers we had to deep-freeze." He looked up, a serious expression on his face. "Don't take that lightly, okay? Plenty of guys here would love to nap through their shifts instead of work. Don't pull that trigger unless you have to."

"I won't."

"Good." Merriman nodded. "I hope you have an uneventful shift. I've got to run before this stuff kicks in." He took another fierce swig, and Troy's cheeks sucked in with distasteful empathy. "Man, that shit's awful."

He walked past Troy, slapped him on the shoulder, and started to reach for the light switch. He stopped himself at the last minute and looked back guiltily, nodded, then was gone.

And just like that, Troy was in charge. His bladder nearly emptied at the thought.

"Hey, wait!" He glanced around the office, hurried out, and caught up with Merriman, who was already turning down the main hall toward the security gate. Troy jogged to catch up.

"You leave the light on?" Merriman asked.

Troy glanced over his shoulder. "Yeah, but—"

"Good habits," Merriman said. He shook his thermos. "Form them."

A heavyset man hurried out of one of the offices and labored to catch up with them. "Merriman! You done with your shift?"

The two men shared a warm handshake. Merriman smiled and nodded. "I am. Troy here will be taking my place."

The man shrugged, didn't introduce himself. "I'm off in two weeks," he said, as if that explained his indifference.

"Look, I'm running late," Merriman said, his eyes darting Troy's direction with a trace of blame. He pushed the thermos into his friend's palm. "Here. You can have what's left." He slapped the man on the arm and turned to go. Troy continued following along.

"No freakin' thanks!" the man called out, waving the thermos and laughing.

Merriman glanced over at Troy. "I'm sorry, did you have a question?" He passed through the turnstile with a click and a metallic thunk. Troy followed. The guard never looked up from his tablet.

"A few, yeah. You mind if I ride down with you? I was a little...late with my orientation. Sudden promotion. Would love to clarify a few things—"

"Hey, I can't stop you. You're in charge." Merriman jabbed the call button on the express.

"So, basically, I'm just here in case something goes wrong?"

The elevator dinged open. Merriman turned and squinted at Troy almost as if to gauge if he was being serious.

"Your job is to *make sure* nothing goes wrong." He stepped into the elevator. Troy followed. Gravity loosened its grip as the car raced downward.

"Right. Of course. That's what I meant."

"You've read the Order, right?"

Troy nodded. *For a different job*, he wanted to say.

"Just follow the script. You'll get questions from the other silos now and then. I found it wise to say as little as possible. Just be quiet and listen. Keep in mind that these are mostly second and third generation survivors, so their vocabulary is already a little different. There's a list of forbidden words in your folder."

Troy felt his head spin. When the elevator slowed and put some weight on his feet, he felt a bout of dizziness and nearly sagged to the ground. He was still incredibly weak.

The door dinged open. He followed Merriman down a short hallway, the same hallway he had emerged from hours earlier. The doctor and his assistant waited in the room beyond, preparing an IV. The doctor looked curiously at Troy as if he hadn't planned on seeing him again so soon, if ever.

"You finish your last meal?" the doctor asked, waving Merriman toward a stool.

"Every vile drop of it." Merriman unclasped the tops of his coveralls and let them flop down around his waist. He sat and held out his arm, palm up. His back was bent with apparent exhaustion, the hair on his chest grayer than on his head. Troy saw how pale Merriman's skin was, the loose tangle of purple lines weaving past his elbow. He tried not to watch the needle go in.

"I'm repeating my notes here," Merriman told him, "but you'll want to meet with Victor in the psych office. He's right across the hall from you. There's some strange things going on in a few of the silos, more fracturing than we thought. Try and get a handle on that for the next guy."

Troy nodded.

"We need to get you to your chamber," the doctor said. His young assistant stood by with a paper gown. The entire procedure looked very familiar. The doctor turned to Troy as if he were a stain that needed scrubbing away.

Troy backed out the door and glanced down the hall in the direction of the deep-freeze. The women and children were kept there, along with the men who couldn't make it through their shifts. "Do you mind if I—?" There was a tug in that direction that he couldn't define. Merriman and the doctor both frowned.

"It's not a good idea—" the doctor began.

"I wouldn't," Merriman said. "I made a few visits the first weeks. It's a mistake. Let it go."

Troy stared wistfully down the hallway. He wasn't exactly sure what he would find there, anyway.

"Get through the next six months," Merriman said. "It goes by fast. It all goes by fast."

Troy nodded. The doctor shooed him away with his eyes while Merriman began tugging off his boots. Troy turned, gave the heavy door down the hall one last glance, then headed the other direction for the lift.

He hoped Merriman was right. Jabbing the button to call the express, he tried to imagine his entire shift flashing by. And the one after that. And the next one. Until this insanity had run its course.

# 5
## 2049 • Washington, D.C.

**T**ime was flying by for Donald Keene. Another day had come to an end, another week, and still he needed more time. It seemed the sun had just gone down when he looked up and it was past eleven.

*Helen.* There was an adrenaline rush of panic as he fumbled for his phone. He had promised his wife he would always call before ten. Tapping her picture on the home screen, he felt a guilty heat wedge around his collar. He imagined her sitting around, staring at her phone, waiting and waiting.

It didn't even ring on his end before she picked up.

"There you are," she said, her voice soft and drowsy, her tone hinting more at relief than anger.

"Sweetheart. God, I'm really sorry. I totally lost track of time."

"That's okay, baby." She yawned, and Donald had to fight the infectious urge to do the same. His jaws cramped from the effort.

"You write any good laws today?" she asked.

He laughed and rubbed his face. "They don't really let me do that. Not yet." His jaw and neck felt constricted from the swallowed yawn. "I'm mostly been staying busy with this little project for the Senator—"

He stopped himself. Donald had dithered all week on the best way to tell her, what parts to keep secret, what was classified. He glanced at the extra monitor on his desk. Anna's perfume was somehow frozen in the air, still lingering a week later.

Helen's voice perked up: "Oh?"

He could picture her clearly, had a sudden satellite image of their neighborhood outside of Savannah, the roof of his house cut away like in a CAD rendering, Helen in her nightgown, his side of the bed still immaculately made, a glass of water within her reach. He missed her terribly. The guilt he felt in spite of his complete innocence made him miss her all the more.

"What does he have you doing? It's legal, I hope."

"What? Of course it's legal. It's...some architectural stuff, actually." Donald leaned forward to grab the finger of gold scotch left in his tumbler. "To be honest, I'd forgotten how much I love the work. I would've been a decent architect if I'd stuck with it." He took a burning sip and eyed his monitors, which had gone dark to save the screens. He was dying to get back to it. Everything fell away, disappeared, when he could lose himself in the drawing.

"Sweetheart, I don't think designing a new bathroom for Mr. Thurman's office is why the taxpayers sent you to Washington."

Donald smiled and finished the drink. He could practically hear his wife grinning on the other end of the line. He set the glass back on his desk and propped up his feet. "It's nothing like that," he insisted, his mouth burning. "It's plans for that facility they're putting in outside of Atlanta. Just a minor portion of it, really. But if I don't get it just right, the whole thing could fall apart."

He eyed the open folder on his desk. His wife laughed sleepily and yawned.

"Why in the world would they have you doing something like that?" she asked. "If it's so important, wouldn't they pay someone who knows what they're doing?"

Donald laughed. "Hey, that hurts. And besides, I'm really good at this—"

"I'm sure you're wonderful at it." His wife yawned again. "But you could've stayed *home* and been an architect. You could work late *here*."

"Yeah, I know." Donald remembered their discussions on whether or not he should run for office, if it would be worth them being apart. Now he was spending his time away doing the very thing they'd agreed he should give up. "I think this is just something they put us through our first year," he said. "It's like hazing us with busywork. It'll get better. And besides, I think it's a *good* sign he wants me in on this. He sees the Atlanta thing as a family project, something to keep in-house. And he actually took notice of my work at—"

"*Family* project."

"Well, not *literally* family, more like—" This wasn't how he wanted to tell her. It was a bad start. It was what he got for putting it off day after day, for waiting until he was exhausted and tipsy.

"Is this why you're working late? Why you're calling me after ten?"

"Baby, I lost track of the time. I was on my computer—" He looked to his glass, saw that it held the barest of sips, just the golden residue that had slid down the tumbler after his last pull. "This is good news for us. I'll be coming home more often because of this. I'm sure they'll need me to check out the job site, work with the foremen—"

"That *would* be good news. Your dog misses you."

Donald smiled. "I hope you *both* do."

"You know I do."

"Good." He tried to fish those last drops out of his glass, was too tired to get up and pour another. "And listen, I know how you're gonna feel about this, and I swear it's out of my control, but the Senator's daughter is working on this project with me. Mick Webb, too. You remember him?"

Cold silence. Donald peered into his empty glass.

"I remember the Senator's daughter," Helen said.

Donald cleared his throat. "Yeah, well, Mick is doing some of the organizational work, securing land, dealing with contractors. It's practically his district, after all. And you know neither of us would be where we are today without the Senator stumping for us—"

"What I remember is that you two used to date. And that she used to flirt with you even when I was around—"

Donald laughed. "Are you serious? Anna Thurman? C'mon, honey, that was a lifetime ago—"

"I thought you were going to come home more often, anyway. On the weekends." He heard his wife let out her breath, the phone rub against her cheek. "Look, it's late. Why don't we both get some sleep? We can talk about this tomorrow."

"Okay. Yeah, sure. And sweetheart?"

She waited.

"Nothing's gonna come between us, okay? This is a huge opportunity for me. And it's something I'm really good at. I'd forgotten how good at it I am."

A pause.

"There's a lot you're good at," his wife said. "You're a good husband, and I know you'll be a good congressman. I just don't trust the people you're surrounding yourself with."

"I understand. But you know I wouldn't be here if it wasn't for him."

"I know."

"Okay. Look, I'll be careful. I promise."

"Hm. Now *that's* one thing you *aren't* all that great at. I'll talk to you tomorrow. Sleep tight. I love you."

She hung up before he could ask what she'd meant. What *wasn't* he good at? Being careful? Or making promises?

He looked down at his phone, saw that he had a dozen emails waiting for him and decided to ignore them until morning. Rubbing his eyes, he tried to will himself to not feel sleepy, to think clearly. He shook the mouse to stir his monitors. They could afford to nap, to go dark a while, but not him.

When they blinked to life, a wireframe apartment sat in the middle of his new screen. Donald spun the wheel on his mouse and watched the apartment sink away and a hallway appear, then dozens of identical wedge-shaped living quarters squeeze in from the edges. The building specs called for a bunker that could house five to ten thousand people for at least a year.

Donald approached the task as he would any design project. He imagined himself in their place, a toxic spill, a leak or some horrible fallout, a terrorist attack, something that might send all the facility workers underground where they would have to stay for weeks or months until the area was cleared.

The view pulled back until another floor appeared above and below, still zooming out, layers sandwiched like cake, empty floors he would eventually fill with storerooms, hallways. There were entire other floors and mechanical shafts left empty for Anna—

"Donny?"

His door opened—the soft knock came after. Donald's arm jerked so hard, his mouse went skidding off the pad and across his desk. He sat up straight, peered over his monitors, and saw Mick Webb grinning at him from the doorway. Mick had his jacket tucked under one arm, tie hanging loose, a peppery stubble on his dark skin. He laughed at the startled expression that must've been plastered across Donald's face and sauntered across the room while Donald fumbled for the mouse and quickly minimized the AutoCAD window.

"Goodness, man, you haven't taken up day trading, have you?"

"Day trading?" Donald leaned back in his chair.

"Yeah. What's with the setup?" Mick walked around behind his desk and rested a hand on the back of his chair. An abandoned game of FreeCell sat embarrassingly on the smaller of the two screens.

"Oh, the extra monitor." He minimized the card game and turned in his seat. "I like having a handful of programs up at the same time."

"I can see that." Mick gestured at the empty monitors, the wallpaper of cherry blossoms framing the Jefferson Memorial.

Donald laughed and rubbed his face. He could feel his own stubble, had forgotten to eat dinner. His stomach had moved right past the empty grumbles and into clenched-fist territory. Surprisingly, he could still hear Margaret in the next room talking on the phone. How much extra work was the distraction of this project costing his secretary? It had only been a week, and already he was a wreck.

"I'm heading out for a drink," Mick told him. "You wanna come?"

"No, I've got a little more to do here."

Mick clasped his shoulder and squeezed until it hurt. "I hate to break it to you, man, but you're gonna have to start over. You bury an ace like that, there's no coming back. C'mon, let's get a drink."

"I can't." Donald twisted out from his friend's grasp and turned to face him. "I wasn't sitting here playing solitaire, man, I was working on those plans for Atlanta. I'm not supposed to let anyone see them. It's top secret."

For emphasis, he reached out and closed the folder on his desk. The Senator had told him there would be a division of labor and that the walls of that divide would need to be a mile high.

"Ohhh. *Top secret*." Mick waggled both hands in the air. "I'm working on the same project, asshole." He waved at the monitor. "And you're doing the plans? What gives? My GPA was higher than yours." He leaned over the desk and stared at the taskbar. "AutoCAD? Cool. C'mon, let's see it."

"Yeah, right."

"Oh, c'mon, Donny. You tell me your secrets, and I'll tell you mine."

Donald laughed. "No way. Look, even the people on my team aren't going to see the entire plan. Neither will I."

"That's dumb."

"No, it's how shit like this gets done. You know how they built the ISS. Each country worked on its own module, and then they hooked them together afterward."

Mick scoffed. "And then it came down in the Pacific."

"Yeah, on *purpose*. And you don't see me prying into your part in all this."

Mick waved a hand dismissively. "Whatever. What you're doing is boring, anyway. Now grab your coat. Let's go."

"Yeah, okay." Donald patted his cheeks with his palms, trying to wake up. "I'll work better in the morning."

"Working on a Saturday. Now *that's* the college spirit!" The slap to his back jolted Donald to his senses.

"Yeah, actually, it's not. Just let me save my work and shut this down."

Mick laughed. "Go ahead. I'm not looking." He made a loose web of fingers over his face, his eyes bugging through the gaps. Donald pointed across the room and waited until his friend had sauntered behind the monitors. He saved his work and shut his computer down.

When he stood, his desk phone rang with full blasts rather than the chirping bursts of being patched through—someone with his direct line. Donald reached for it and held up a finger for Mick.

"Helen—?"

Someone cleared their throat on the other end. A deep and rough voice apologized. "Sorry, no."

"Oh." Donald glanced up at Mick, who was checking out the spines on his bookshelf. "Hello, sir."

"You boys going out?" Senator Thurman asked.

Donald swallowed and turned toward the window. "Excuse me?"

"You and Mick. It's a Friday night. Are you hitting the town?"

"Uh, just one drink, sir. Catch up with a college buddy, you know?"

What Donald wanted to know was how the hell the Senator knew Mick was there. He decided his receptionist must have taken the call and told Thurman to try him direct.

"Good. Tell Mick I need to see him first thing Monday morning. My office. You, too. We need to discuss your first trip down to the job site."

"Oh. Okay."

Donald waited, wondering if that was all.

"You boys will be working closely on this moving forward."

"Good. Of course."

Mick turned and jerked his head toward the door. Donald held up a finger.

"As we discussed last week, there won't be any need to share details about what you're working on with other project members. The same goes for Mick."

"Yessir. Absolutely. I remember our talk."

"Excellent. You boys have a good time. Oh, and if Mick starts blabbing, you have my permission to kill him on the spot."

There was a breath of silence, and then the hearty laugh of a man whose lungs were much younger than his years.

"Ah." Donald watched Mick lift the plug from a decanter and take a sniff. "Okay, sir. Good one. I'll be sure to do that."

"Great. See you Monday."

There was a click. The Senator had hung up before Donald could force himself to laugh. As he returned the phone to its cradle and grabbed his coat, his new monitor remained quietly perched on his desk, watching him blankly.

# 6
2110 • Silo 1

Troy's beat-up plastic meal tray slid down the line behind the splattered sheet of glass. Once his badge was scanned, a measured portion of canned string beans fell out of a tube and formed a steaming pile on his plate. A perfectly round cut of turkey plopped from the next tube, the ridges still visible from the tin. Mashed potatoes spat out at the end of the line like a spit wad from a child's straw. Gravy followed with a well-aimed squirt.

Behind the serving line, a man in white coveralls with a white beard stood emotionless, hands clasped behind his back. He didn't seem interested in the food. He watched the workers as they lined up for their meals, appeared to be more keen on them.

When Troy's tray reached the end of the line, a young man, also in white and probably not out of his twenties, arranged silverware and napkins by the plate. A glass of water was added from a nearby tray tightly arranged with them. The final step was like a ritualized handshake, one Troy remembered from the months of orientation: a small plastic shot glass was handed over, a pill rattling in the bottom, a blurry blue shape barely visible through the translucent cup.

The gentleman ahead of Troy accepted his tray and cup. Tilting his head back, he shook the plastic cup, and the blue blur skittered a short hop past his lips. The man took a quick sip of water before grabbing his tray and finding a place to eat.

Troy shuffled into place.

"Hello, sir."

A young grin. Perfect teeth. Everyone called him sir, even those much older. It was discomfiting no matter who it came from.

The pill rattled in the plastic. Troy accepted the cup and tossed it down. He swallowed it dry, grabbed his tray, and tried not to hold up the line. Searching for a seat, he caught the man with the white beard watching him. Everyone in the facility seemed to think Troy was in charge, but Troy wasn't fooled. He was just another person doing a job, following a script. Sometimes, he wondered if anyone sat at the end of the line or if it was all a big circle of confusion.

He found an empty spot facing the view. Unlike that first day, it didn't bother him to see out. He found it comforting. He remembered a man crying on the lift that same day, wondered if that fellow was feeling better now.

A scoop of potatoes and gravy washed away the bitter taste of the pill. Mere water was never up to the task. Eating methodically, he watched the sun set on the first week of his first shift. Twenty-five more weeks to go. It was a countable number. It felt much shorter than half a year. Switching to days, he had one hundred seventy-six remaining. That seemed like a lot. How one framed things really mattered.

An older gentleman sat down diagonally across from him, polite enough to not block the view. Troy recognized the man, had spoken with him once by the recycling bin. When the gentleman looked up, Troy nodded in greeting.

They ate.

The cafeteria hummed with a pleasant sound. Plastic, glass, and metal beat a rhythmless tune. A few hushed conversations rose and faded. Troy spent a lot of time gazing past the rotting debris and up at the hills.

Breakfast and dinner were his favorite hours. Lunch was delivered to his office, which left him trapped in the middle of the building. He didn't like the middle. There was nothing calling to him there. It was a place of being torn between two longings—the hard-to-define urge to unbury himself in the cafeteria, and a darker beckoning that called to him from below.

There were things he was supposed to know, but he kept forgetting. He awoke each morning with them in his vision, could feel memories taking shape, but by breakfast they were fading. By dinner, they were dull aches. It left Troy with a general sadness, a cold sensation and a feeling like a hollow stomach—different from hunger—like rainy days as a child when he didn't know what to do with his time. It was the pain of a chronic boredom mixed with the discomfort of time wasted.

He scraped the last of his potatoes off his tray. The gentleman across from him slid over a little and cleared his throat. Troy glanced up and slid the potatoes off the fork with his teeth, his arms erupting in gooseflesh from the sound and taste of metal scraping on enamel.

The old man smiled. "Things going okay?" he asked.

He reminded Troy of someone. Blotchy skin hung slightly loose around his face. He had the drooping neck, that pinch of flesh hanging from his Adam's apple that made old people look like they were melting.

"What things?" Troy asked. He returned the smile and looked back to his plate. The knife was superfluous. Hardly any weight with the edge of his fork, and an unnatural bite of turkey slid off from the rest.

"Anything, I suppose. Just checking in. I go by Hal." The gentleman lifted his glass. Troy did the same. It was as good as a handshake.

"Troy," he said. He supposed to some people it still mattered what they called themselves.

Hal took a long pull from his glass. His neck bobbed, the gulp loud. Self-conscious, Troy took a small sip and worked on the last of his beans and turkey.

"I've noticed some people sit facing it and some sit with their backs to it." Hal jerked his thumb over his shoulder.

Troy looked up at the screen. He chewed his food, didn't say anything.

"I reckon those who sit and watch, there's something they're trying to remember."

Troy froze. He swallowed and forced himself to shrug.

"And some of us who don't want to see, I figure we're trying our best to forget."

Troy swallowed the last of his water, had rationed poorly. He still had a few bites of beans left. Something told him they shouldn't be having this conversation.

"It's the bad stuff," Hal said, staring off toward the elevators. "Have you noticed that? It's just the bad stuff that slips away. Anything that don't matter all that much just sits there."

Troy jabbed his beans even though he didn't plan on eating them.

"It makes you wonder, don't it?"

Looking up at the screen, Troy saw that the hills were almost invisible. They were turning the same color of darkness as the evening and cloud-filled sky.

"Makes you wonder why we all feel so rotten inside." Hal took a bite of his potatoes.

Troy watched the man chew, jowls quivering. He eventually scraped the green beans off his fork, looked down at them, then jabbed them a second time.

# 7
2049 • Washington, D.C.

**D**onald was glad he had decided to walk to his meeting with the Senator. The rain from the week before had finally let up, and the traffic in Dupont Circle was at a crawl. As he skirted the park and left Johns Hopkins behind—the sidewalks there packed with young men and women in scrubs, both hands wrapped around their Starbucks—he saw in the circle's traffic a metaphor for the city.

Ten streets to choose from, ten routes colliding without compromise. There was the honking and the shaking of fists, no one willing to merge. The tourists were trapped in the inner lanes; they went around and around and got nowhere. Here was Washington encapsulated as far as Donald was concerned. It was as though he had the same two choices: he could spin in circles, completely lost and doing little, or he could dive down one avenue and forsake the others, always fearing he'd picked poorly. So far, he had tended toward the latter with few regrets.

A taxi driver close to the curb laid on his horn. These were like the lobbyists in Rayburn, the real experts who knew the backstreets. They probably wished these tourists would just vanish so they could get around without all the delays.

Heading up Connecticut and leaning into a stiffening breeze, Donald wondered why his meeting with the Senator had been moved to Kramer's Bookshop of all places. There were a dozen superior coffee joints half the distance away.

He crossed a side street and hurried up the short flight of stone steps to the bookshop. The front door to Kramer's was one of those ancient wooden affairs older establishments hung like a boast, like a testament to their endurance. He pushed it open and ducked inside as a fresh gust blew grit and fluttering trash down Connecticut Avenue.

Hinges squeaked and actual bells jangled overhead. Donald wiped his feet on the welcome mat and turned to close the door behind him—an act as foreign and quaint as it might feel to eat with one's hands. The bells jangled a second time as the top of the door knocked into them, and a young woman straightening books on a center table of bestsellers glanced up and smiled hello.

The café, Donald saw, was packed with men and women in business suits, white porcelain cups rising and falling, an espresso machine releasing a deathly wail as it steamed someone's milk. He returned the warm smile as the bookseller continued arranging the hardbacks. There was no sign of the Senator in the cafe. Donald started to check his phone, see if he was too early, when a Secret Service agent caught his eye.

The agent stood broad-shouldered at the end of an aisle of physical books in the small corner of Kramer's that had not yet succumbed to the café. Donald laughed at how conspicuously hidden the man was. Their ilk seemed to get a kick out of dressing up overly normal and then flashing their earpieces, the bulges by their ribs, and the ubiquitous sunglasses. Skirting the table of bestsellers, Donald headed the agent's way, admiring the wide planks underfoot that chased him with the squeaks and groans of age.

There was an irrational urge to hold his hands up in submission as he approached the agent. Donald had been around a few who came across as twitchy. The agent's gaze shifted his way, but it was hard to tell if he was looking at Donald or just generally toward the front door.

"I'm here to see Senator Thurman," he said, his voice cracking a little. "I have an appointment."

The agent turned his head to the side. Donald followed the gesture and peered down an aisle of books to see Thurman browsing through the stacks at the far end.

"Ah. Thanks." He assumed he was free to pass, that he wouldn't get shot in the back or tased. He reluctantly tested the theory as he stepped between the towering shelves of old books, the light dimming and the smell of coffee replaced with the tang of mildew mixed with leather.

"What do you think of this one?"

Senator Thurman held out a book as Donald approached. No greeting, just a question. As if Donald had been standing there all along.

Donald checked the title embossed in gold on the thick leather cover. "Never heard of it," he admitted.

Senator Thurman laughed. "Of course not. It's over a hundred years old—and it's French. I mean, what do you think of the *binding*." He handed Donald the book.

Donald accepted it and was surprised by how heavy the volume was. He cracked it open and flipped through a few pages. It felt like a law book, had that same dense heft, but he could see by the whitespace between lines of dialog that it was a novel. As he turned a few pages, he admired how thin the individual sheets were, each one smooth as silk. Where the pages met at the spine, they had been stitched together with tiny ropes of blue and gold thread. He had friends who still swore by physical books—not to decorate with but to actually read. Studying the one in his hand, Donald caught a whiff of their affection, could understand what they were getting at.

"The binding looks great," he said, brushing it with the pads of his fingers. It was like admiring an aesthetically pleasing and well-designed building. "It's a beautiful book." He handed the novel back to the Senator. "Is this how you shop for a good read? You mostly go by the cover?"

Thurman tucked the book under his arm and pulled another from the shelf. "It's just a sample for another project I'm working on." He turned and narrowed his eyes at Donald. It was an uncomfortable gaze to be at the wrong end of. He felt like prey, like a wounded beast leaving a glaring trail with every word and twitch. A clumsy sentence snapped a twig here, a bad joke dripped a spot of blood there. He was trying so hard to manage the man's impression of him, and yet it felt as though the Senator could track him down with every utterance.

"How's your sister doing?" Thurman asked.

The question caught Donald off guard. A lump formed in his throat at the mention of her.

"Charlotte? She's...she's fine, I guess. She redeployed. I'm sure you heard."

"I did." Thurman slotted the book in his hand back into a gap and weighed the one Donald had appraised. "I was proud of her for re-upping. She does her country proud."

Donald thought about what it cost a family to do a country proud.

"Yeah," he said. "I mean, I know my parents were really looking forward to having her home, but she was having trouble adjusting to the pace back here. It...I don't think she'll be able to really *relax* until the war's over. You know?"

"I do. And she may not find peace even then."

That wasn't what Donald wanted to hear. He watched the Senator trace his finger down an ornate spine adorned with ridges, bumps, and recessed lettering. The old man's eyes seemed to focus beyond the rows of books.

"I can drop her a line if you want. Sometimes a soldier just needs to hear that it's okay to see someone."

"If you mean a shrink, she won't do it." Donald remembered Charlotte before and after the sessions. "We already tried."

Thurman's lips pursed into a thin, wrinkled line, his worry revealed in hidden signs of age. "I'll talk to her. I'm familiar enough with the hubris of youth, believe me. I used to have the same attitude when I was younger." He touched another book. "I thought I didn't need any help, that I could do everything on my own." He turned to face Donald. "The profession's come a long way. They have pills now that can help her with the battle fatigue."

Donald shook his head. "No. She was on those for a while. They made her forget too much. And they caused a—" He hesitated, didn't want to talk about it. "—a *tic*."

He wanted to say tremors, but that sounded too severe. And while he appreciated the Senator's concern—this feeling again like the man was family—he felt uncomfortable discussing his sister's problems. He remembered the last time she was home, the disagreement they'd had while going through his and Helen's photographs from Mexico. He had asked her if she remembered Cozumel from when they were kids, and Charlotte had insisted she'd never been. The disagreement had turned into an argument, and he had lied and said his eventual tears were ones of frustration. Parts of his sister's life had been erased, and all the doctors could say to explain it was that it must've been something she *wanted* to forget, and what could be wrong with that?

Thurman rested a hand on Donald's arm. "Trust me on this," he said quietly. "I'll talk to her. I know what she's going through."

Donald bobbed his head. "Yeah. Okay. I appreciate it." He almost added that it wouldn't do any good, could possibly cause harm, but the gesture was a nice one. And it would come from someone his sister looked up to rather than from family.

"And hey, Donny, she's piloting drones." Thurman studied him, seemed to be picking up on his worry. "It's not like she's in any physical danger."

Donald rubbed the spine of a shelved book. "Not physical, no."

The conversation fell silent, and Donald let out a heavy breath. The wail of the espresso machine leaked through the wall of ancient books. He could hear the chatter from the café, the clink of a spoon stirring in some sugar, the clang of bells against the old wooden door, hinges squealing.

He had seen videos of what Charlotte did, camera feeds from the drones and then from the missiles as they were guided into their targets. The video quality was amazing. You could see people turning to look up toward the heavens in surprise, could see the last moments of their lives, could tick through the shots frame by frame and decide—*after the fact*—if this had been your man or not. He knew what his sister did, what she went through.

Bells rang and hinges squealed as an old door was closed again.

"I spoke with Mick earlier," Thurman said, seeming to sense that he'd brought up a sore topic. "You two are going to head down to Atlanta and see how the excavation is going."

Donald snapped to. "Of course. Yeah, it'll be good to get the lay of the land. I got a nice head start on my plans last week, gradually filling in the dimensions you set out. You do realize how deep this thing goes, right?"

"That's why they're already digging the foundations. The outer walls should be getting a pour over the next few weeks." Senator Thurman patted Donald's shoulder and nodded toward the end of the aisle, signaling that they were done looking through books.

"Wait. They're already *digging*?" Donald walked alongside Thurman. "I've really only got an outline of my structure. I hope they're saving mine for last."

"The entire complex is being worked on at the same time. And all they're pouring are the outer walls and foundations, the dimensions of which have already been settled on in committee. We'll fill each structure from the bottom up, the floors craned down completely furnished before we pour the slabs between. But look, this is why I need you boys to go check things out. It sounds like a damned nightmare down there with the staging. I've got a hundred crews from a dozen countries working on top of each other while materials pile up everywhere. I can't be in ten places at once, so I need you to get a bead on things and report back."

When they reached the Secret Service agent at the end of the aisle, the Senator handed him the old book with the French embossing. The man in the dark shades nodded, reached inside his coat for the smaller of two bulges, and headed toward the counter. Donald watched as the agent stood in line behind customers gazing up at a chalkboard to prepare their orders. There was something comical about him waiting there with that French book, doing the Senator's shopping for him.

"While you're down there," Thurman said, "I want you to meet up with Charlie Rhodes. He's handling delivery of most of the building materials. See if he needs anything."

"*Charles* Rhodes? As in the governor of Oklahoma?"

"That's right. We served together. And hey, I'm working on transitioning you and Mick into some of the higher levels of this project. Our leadership team is still short a few dozen members. So keep up the good work. You've impressed some important people with what you've put together so far, and Anna seems confident you'll be able to stay ahead of schedule. She says the two of you make a great team."

Donald nodded. He felt a blush of pride—and also the sinking feeling of extra responsibilities, more bites out of his ever-dwindling time. Helen wouldn't like hearing that his involvement with the project might grow. In fact, Mick and Anna might be the only people he could share the news with, the only ones he could talk to. Every stupid detail about the build seemed to require convoluted layers of clearance. He couldn't tell if it was the fear of nuclear waste, the threat of terrorist attack, or the likelihood that the project would fall through. Everything for their political party seemed to hinge on this. Across the aisle, lips were chapped from all the licking going on at the prospect of failure. It created a situation where it was better to keep mum than risk being the one who blew it.

The agent returned and took up a position beside the Senator, shopping bag in hand. Donald had the feeling that someone was watching him, then and always. It reinforced the need to keep quiet. He didn't even know who was seeing the plans he was working on; Thurman said others were impressed with his work, but he'd only sent partial files to Anna.

The agent studied him through those impenetrable sunglasses. Donald wondered if they had access to his computer—and whether it mattered. The files were *for* them, anyway.

Senator Thurman shook Donald's hand and said to keep him posted. Another agent materialized from nowhere and formed up on Thurman's flank. Donald felt a flush of heat as the two men marched the Senator through the jangling door.

Damn the secrets and the intrigue. He cursed the need for them. Donald wished he could just call his wife and let her know about his day, his job, what he was working on. Standing there in that bustling hive of a bookstore-turned-coffee shop, he considered the web of deceit and misdirection being spun in every direction, how a few slender threads could grow outward from seemingly innocent beginnings.

He already felt caught up in it, keeping things from his family, from his secretary—even from Mick, his only real friend on the Hill. He had wandered with innocence and naïveté into the grip of a web, and now every move would wrap him tighter, each lie sticking to the others, until one day he would find himself in a tight little cocoon, trapped and suffocating from the thousands of little fibs that living and working in that cursed swamp of a city seemed to require every man to ooze.

# 8
2110 • Silo 1

The Book of the Order lay open on his desk, the pages curling up from a spine stitched to last. Troy studied the upcoming procedure once again, his first official act as head of Operation Fifty, and it brought to mind a ribbon-cutting ceremony, a grand display where the man with the shears took credit for the hard work of others.

The Order, he had decided, was more recipe book than operations manual. The shrinks who wrote it had accounted for everything. And like the field of psychology, or any field that involved human nature, the things that made no sense usually served some deeper purpose.

It made Troy wonder what *his* purpose was. How necessary was his position? He had studied for a much different job, had been promoted at the last minute, and somehow that made him feel arbitrary. Anyone could be slotted into his place.

Of course, even if his office was mostly titular in nature, perhaps it served some symbolic purpose. Maybe he wasn't there to lead so much as to provide an illusion to the others that *they were being led.*

This was a terrifying thought. Troy imagined the great ship he was helming, this long night shift of six months duration, all of humanity crammed onboard. He could spin the spoked wheel and feel that the linkage to the rudder had been lost. But his job was to turn it nonetheless, to gaze over the bow and pretend that all was in hand as the swell and foam of human nature tossed them to and fro. The deckhands, seeing him at the helm, could then coil lines and trim sheets and sleep soundly in their bunks.

Troy skipped back two paragraphs in the Order. His eyes had looked at every word, but none of them had registered. Everything about his new life made him prone to distraction, made him think too much. It had all been perfectly arranged, but for what? Maximum *apathy*?

Glancing up, he could see Victor sitting at his desk in the psych office across the hall. It would be easy enough to walk over there and ask. They, more than anyone else, had designed this place. He could ask them how they did it, how they managed to make everyone feel so empty inside.

Sheltering the women and the children played some part, Troy was sure of that. The women and children of his silo had been gifted with the long sleep, had been whisked into lifeboats while the men stayed and took shifts steering that gutted wreckage off the icebergs. It removed the passion from the plans, forestalled the chance that the men might fight amongst themselves.

Troy wondered if two bull elk had ever butted heads without a doe watching from a grassy rise. What would be the point?

And then there was the routine, the mind-numbing routine. It was a castration of thought. Like the daily grind of an office worker who drooled at the clock, punched out, watched TV until sleep overtook him, slapped an alarm three times, did it again. It was made worse by the absence of weekends. There were no free days. It was six months on and *decades* off. It made him envious of the rest of the facility, all the other silos, where hallways must echo with the laughter of children, the voices of women, the passion and happiness missing from this singular bunker at the heart of it all.

Checking the clock on his computer, Troy saw that it was time to go. He closed his copy of the Order and locked it away in his desk. As he headed for the communications room, he considered the office building analogy and realized it didn't quite cover it. There was something else. The word that summed up the place was on the tip of his tongue. He tried to puzzle it out as he shuffled down the hall.

It had something to do with the stupor he saw everywhere, with the daily pills in the little plastic cups, the dozens of communal rooms with movies playing in loops on flat-panel TVs, dozens of unblinking eyes in comfortable chairs, staring.

No one was truly awake. Not really. It was just different types of sleep. And by the time Troy got to the end of the hallway, he had his finger on it. He remembered who designed this place, who had *really* laid out the plans. It was the shrinks. They had built a goddamn insane asylum. The world wasn't being steered by a rudderless captain—it was being run from a loony bin! The entire world and everyone in it.

As he entered the comm room, Troy wasn't sure if he should laugh or cry at the realization. Then he remembered how the world was run *before*, and that nothing had really changed. This caused him to chuckle sadly.

A pair of heads turned from the radio stations as he walked in, frowns and lowered brows. Troy pulled himself together. This wasn't an asylum, he lied to himself. This was an office. It was a job. Everything was all right. He just had to keep his shit together. He was there to cut a ribbon.

Saul, one of the lead radio techs, took off his headset and rose to greet him. Troy vaguely knew Saul; they lived on the same executive wing and saw each other in the gym from time to time. While they shook hands, Saul's wide and handsome face tickled some deeper memory, an itch Troy had learned to ignore. Maybe this was someone he knew from his orientation, from before his long sleep.

Saul introduced him to the other tech, who waved and kept his headset on. The name would probably fade immediately. It didn't matter. An extra headset was pulled from a rack. Troy accepted it and lowered it around his neck, keeping the muffs off his ears so he could still hear. Saul found the silvery jack at the end of the headset and ran his fingers across a wide array of empty receptacles. The layout and the room reminded Troy of ancient photographs of phone operators back before they were replaced with computers and automated voices.

The mental image of a bygone day mixed and fizzed with his nerves and the shivers brought on by the pills, and Troy felt a sudden bout of giggles bubble beneath the surface. The laughter nearly burst out of him, but he managed to hold it together. It probably wouldn't be a good sign for the head of overall operations to lurch into hysterics when he was about to gauge the fitness of a future silo head.

"—and you'll just run through the set questions," Saul was telling him. He held out a plastic card to Troy, who was pretty sure he didn't need it but took it anyway. He'd been memorizing the routine for most of the day. Besides, he was quite sure it didn't matter what he said. Like the phone operators of old, the task of gauging fitness was better left to the machines and the computers, all the sensors in some distant headset.

"Okay. There's the call." Saul pointed to a single flashing light on a panel studded with flashing lights. The entire *room* was full of flashing lights. Troy was surprised any sort of alert stood out to these men. They reminded him of those expert astronomers who could glance up at the night sky and spot a distant supernova, could see a new pinprick that was out of place among all the others.

"I'm patching you through," Saul said.

Troy adjusted the muffs around his ears as the tech made the connection. He heard a few beeps before the line clicked over. Someone was breathing on the other side. Troy reminded himself that this young man would be far more nervous than he was. After all, he had to *answer* the questions—Troy simply had to ask them.

He glanced down at the card in his hand, his mind suddenly blank, thankful that he'd been given the thing.

"Name?" he asked the young man.

"Marcus Dent, sir."

There was a quiet confidence in the voice, the sound of a chest thrust out with pride, a young man proudly reporting for duty. Troy remembered feeling that once, a long time ago. And then he thought of the world Marcus Dent had been born into, a legacy *he* would only ever know from books.

"Tell me about your training," Troy said, reading the lines. He tried to keep his voice even, deep, full of command. Saul made a hoop with his finger and thumb, letting him know he was getting good data from the boy's headset. Troy wondered if his was similarly equipped. Could anyone in that room—or any other room—tell how nervous he was?

"Well, sir, I shadowed under Deputy Willis before transferring to IT Security. That was a year ago. I've been studying the Order for six weeks. I feel ready, sir."

Shadowing. Troy forgot it was called that. He had meant to bring the latest vocabulary card with him but forgot.

"What is your primary duty to the…silo?" He had nearly said *facility*.

"To maintain the Order, sir."

"And what do you protect above all?"

He kept his voice flat. The best readings would come from not imparting too much emotion into the man being measured.

"Life and Legacy," Marcus recited.

Troy had a difficult time seeing the next question. It was obscured by an unexpected blur of tears. His hand trembled. He lowered the shaking card to his side before anyone noticed.

"And what does it take to protect the things we hold dear?" he asked. His voice sounded like someone else's. He ground his teeth together to keep them from chattering. Something was wrong with him. Something powerfully wrong.

"Sacrifice," Marcus said, steady as a rock.

Troy blinked rapidly to clear his vision, and Saul held up his hand to let him know he could continue, that the measures were coming through. Now they needed baselines so the biometrics could tease out the boy's sincerity toward the first questions. In the old days, this was when they asked your name on a lie detector to establish a normal response. Troy's palms felt sweaty thinking of someone hooking him up to a machine and asking him his name.

"Tell me, Marcus, do you have a girlfriend?"

He didn't know why that was the first thing that came to mind. Maybe it was the envy that other silos didn't freeze their women, didn't freeze anyone at all. Nobody in the comm room seemed to react or care. The formal portion of the test was over.

"Oh, yessir," Marcus said, and Troy heard the boy's breathing change, could imagine his body unstiffening. "We've applied to be married, sir. Just waiting to hear back."

"Well, I don't think you'll have to wait too much longer. What's her name?"

"Melanie, sir. She works here in IT."

"That's great." Troy wiped at his eyes. The shivers seemed to have passed. Saul waved his finger in a circle over his head, letting him know he could wrap it up. They had enough.

"Marcus Dent," he said, "welcome to Operation Fifty of the World Order."

"Thank you, sir." The young man's voice dripped with pride.

There was a pause, then the sound of a deep breath taken and held.

"Sir? Is it okay if I ask a question?"

Troy looked to the others. There were shrugs and not much else in the way of direction. He considered the role this young man had just assumed, remembered feeling daunted in his last job, that mix of fear, eagerness, and confusion.

"Sure, son. One question." He figured he was in charge. He could make a few rules of his own.

Marcus cleared his throat. Troy pictured him and the current head of the silo sitting in a room together, master studying student.

"I lost my grandmother a few years ago," Marcus said. "She used to let slip little things about the world before. Not in a forbidden way, but just as a product of her dementia. The doctors said she was resistant to her medication."

Troy didn't like the sound of this, that third-generation survivors were gleaning anything about the past. Marcus may be newly cleared for such things, but others weren't.

"What's your question?" Troy asked.

"The Legacy, sir. I've done some reading in it as well, not neglecting my studies of the Order and the Pact, of course, and there's something I have to know."

Another deep breath.

"Is everything in the Legacy true?"

Troy thought about this. He considered the great collection of books that contained the world's history, a carefully edited history. In his mind, he could see the leather spines and the gilded pages, the rows and rows of books they had been shown during their orientation.

He nodded and found himself once again needing to wipe his eyes.

"Yes," he told Marcus, his voice dry and flat. "It's true."

Someone in the room sniffled. Troy knew the ceremony had gone on long enough. The muffs were hot against his skin.

"Everything in there is absolutely true," he said.

Which was partially correct. He didn't add that not every *true thing* was written in the Legacy. Much was left out. And there were other things he suspected that *none* of them knew, things that had been wiped clean, had been edited out of books and brains alike.

The Legacy was the truth allowed, he wanted to say, the truth that was carried in all the silos for future generations. But the lies, he thought to himself, were what they carried there in Silo 1, in that drug-hazed asylum charged insanely with humanity's survival.

# 9
## 2049 • Fulton County, Georgia

The front-end loader let out a throaty blat as it struggled up the hill. When it reached the top, a charcoal geyser of relief streamed from its exhaust pipe, a load of dirt avalanched out of its toothy bucket, and Donald saw that the loader wasn't rumbling *up* the hill so much as *creating* it.

Hills of fresh dirt were taking shape like this as far as he could see. Heavy machinery skittered like an infestation of ants, each one carrying a mouthful of dirt at a time and beeping to one another in audible pheromones as they occasionally backed up. Their tracks crisscrossed through the soil in a knot of furrows, angry engines whining, smokestacks belching.

Between the hills—through temporary gaps left open like an ordered maze—burdened dump trucks carried soil and rock from the cavernous pits being hollowed from the earth. These gaps, Donald knew from the topo plans, would one day be pushed closed, leaving little more than a shallow crease where each hill met its neighbor.

Standing on one of these growing mounds, Donald watched the choreographed ballet of heavy machinery while Mick Webb spoke with a contractor about the delays. In their white shirts and flapping ties, the two congressmen seemed incongruous. The men in hardhats with the leather faces, calloused hands, and busted knuckles belonged. He and Mick, blazers tucked under their arms, sweat stains spreading in the humid Georgia heat, were aliens from another land that were somehow—nominally at least—supposed to be in charge of this ungodly commotion.

Another loader released a bite of soil as Donald shifted his gaze toward downtown Atlanta. Past the massive clearing of rising hills and over the treetops still denuded from fading winter rose the glass and steel spires of the old Southern city. An entire corner of sparsely populated Fulton County had been cleared. Remnants of a golf course were still visible at one end where the machines had yet to disturb the land. A pile of stripped trees was being craned onto trucks by a machine with a maw like a beetle's.

Down the slope of that first hill, near the main parking lot, a staging zone the size of several football fields held thousands of shipping containers packed with building supplies, more than Donald thought necessary. But he was learning by the hour that this was the way of government projects, where public expectations were as high as the spending limits. Everything was done in excess or not at all. The plans he had been ordered to draw up practically begged for proportions of insanity, and his wasn't even a necessary component of the facility, not really.

Between Donald and the field of shipping containers stood another impressive array of boxes: trailers, a few used as offices but most of them serving as housing. They formed a temporary city built for thousands. This was where men—

and a handful of women—could ditch their hard hats, where everyone lived in pre-fabbed cans like sardines that had been salted and packed away for later.

Flags flew over many of the trailers, the workforce as multinational as an Olympic Village. Spent nuclear fuel rods from the world over would one day end up buried beneath the pristine soil of Fulton County. It meant that the world had a stake in the project's success. The logistical nightmare this ensured seemed to matter little to the back-room dealers. He and Mick were finding that many of the early construction delays could be traced to language barriers, as neighboring work crews couldn't communicate with each other and had evidently given up trying. Everyone simply worked on their set of plans, heads down, ignoring the rest.

Donald watched them in the distance. Their colorful helmets lent them the appearance of the Lego men he had played with as a kid. And all around them, huge diesel-burning trucks rumbled throughout the encampment, their beds full of work crews and building supplies. One group of men with tiny tubes of paper in their fists kicked through the dust together, and Donald wondered if any of those plans were his own.

Beside this temporary city sat the vast parking lot he and Mick had trudged up from. He could see their rental car down there, the only quiet and electric thing in sight. Small and silver, it seemed to cower among the square-shouldered and belching ogres on all sides. Donald laughed at the sight of it. The overmatched car looked precisely how he felt, both on that little hill at the construction site and back at the Capital one in Washington.

"Two months behind."

Mick smacked him on the arm with his clipboard. "Hey, did you hear me? Two months behind already, and they just broke ground six months ago. How is that even possible?"

Donald had no idea. He shrugged as they left the frowning foremen and trudged down the hill toward the parking lot.

"Maybe because they have elected officials pretending to do jobs that belong to the private sector?" Donald offered, dejectedly.

Mick laughed and squeezed his shoulder. "Jesus, Donny, you sound like a goddamned Republican!"

"Yeah? Well, I feel like we're in over our heads, here." He waved his arm at the depression in the hills they were skirting, a deep bowl scooped out of the earth. Several mixer trucks were pouring concrete into the wide hole at its center. More trucks waited in a line, their butts spinning impatiently.

"You do realize," Donald said, "that one of these holes is going to hold plans they let *me* draw up, right? Doesn't that spook you? All this money? It freaks me out."

Mick's fingers dug painfully into Donald's neck. His friend laughed over the rumbling, beeping machines.

"I'm being serious," Donald said. "Billions of taxpayer dollars are gonna nestle in the dirt out there in the shape that *I* drew up. It seemed so...*abstract* before."

"Christ, don't be so melodramatic. This isn't about you or your plans." He popped Donald with the clipboard and used it to point toward the container field. Through a fog of dust, a large man in a cowboy hat was waving them over. "Besides," Mick said, as they angled away from the parking lot, "what're the chances anyone even uses your little bunker? This is about energy independence. It's about the death of coal. You know, it feels like the rest of us are building a nice big house over here, and you're over in a corner stressing about where you're gonna hang the fire extinguisher—"

"*Little bunker?*" Donald held his blazer up over his mouth as the cloud of dust blew across them. "Do you know how many floors *deep* this thing is gonna be? If you set it on the ground, it'd be the tallest building in the world—!"

Mick laughed. "Not for long it wouldn't. Not if you designed it. It'd be the tallest pile of *rubble* in the world."

Donald didn't find this nor Mick's nonchalance amusing. The man in the cowboy hat drew closer. He smiled as he kicked through the packed dirt to meet them, and Donald finally recognized him from TV: Charles Rhodes, the governor of Oklahoma.

"You need to keep some perspective," Mick added under his breath. "How many bunkers has this country seen that were never used? Not even once? So relax. You're stressing me out."

"You Senator Thawman's boys?"

Governor Rhodes smiled. He had the authentic drawl to go with the authentic hat, the authentic boots, and the authentic buckle. He rested his hands on his hips, a clipboard in one of them.

Mick nodded. "Yessir. I'm Congressman Webb. This is Congressman Keene."

The two men shook hands. Donald was next. "Governor," he said.

"Got your delivery." He pointed the clipboard back toward the staging area. "Just shy of a hundred containers. Should have somethin' rollin' in about every week. Need one of you to sign right here."

Mick reached out and took the clipboard. Donald saw an opportunity to ask something about Senator Thurman, something he figured an old war buddy would know.

"Why do some people call him that?"

Governor Rhodes laughed. "You mean *Thaw*-man?"

"Yeah."

Mick flipped through the delivery report, a breeze pinning back the pages for him.

"I've heard others call him that when he wasn't around," Donald explained, "but I've been too scared to ask."

Mick looked up from the report with a grin. "It's because he was an ice-cold killer in the war, right?"

Donald cringed. Governor Rhodes laughed.

"Unrelated," he said. "True, but unrelated."

The governor glanced back and forth between them. Mick passed the clipboard to Donald, tapped a page that dealt with the emergency housing facility. Donald looked over the materials list.

"You boys familiar with his anti-cryo bill?" Governor Rhodes asked. He handed Donald a pen, seemed to expect him to just sign the thing and not look over it too closely.

Mick shook his head and shielded his eyes against the Georgia sun. "Anti-cryo?" he asked.

"Yeah. Aw, hell, this probably dates back before you squirts were even born. Senator Thawman penned the bill that put down that cryo fad. Made it illegal to take advantage of rich folk and turn them into ice cubes. It went to the big court, where they voted five-four, and suddenly tens of thousands of popsicles with more money than sense were thawed out and buried proper. These were people, mind you, who'd frozen themselves in the hopes that doctors from the future would discover some medical procedure for extracting their rich heads from their own rich asses!"

The Governor laughed at his own joke, and Mick joined him. A line on the delivery report caught Donald's eye. He turned the clipboard around and showed the governor. "Uh, this shows two thousand spools of fiber-optic. I'm pretty sure my plans call for forty spools."

"Lemme see." Governor Rhodes took the clipboard and procured another pen from his pocket. He clicked the top of it three times, then scratched out the quantity. He wrote in a new number to the side.

"Wait, will the price reflect that?"

"Price is the same," he said. "Just sign the bottom."

"But—"

"Son, this is why hammers cost the Pentagon their weight in gold. It's government accounting. Just a signature, please."

"But that's *fifty times* more fiber than we'll need," Donald complained, even as he found himself scribbling his name. He passed the clipboard to Mick, who signed for the rest of the goods.

"Oh, that's all right." Rhodes took the clipboard and pinched the brim of his hat. "I'm sure they'll find a use for it somewhere."

"Hey, you know," Mick said, "I remember that cryo bill. From law school. There were lawsuits, weren't there? Didn't a group of families bring murder charges against the Feds?"

The governor laughed. "Yeah, but it didn't get far. Hard to prove you killed people who'd already been pronounced dead. And then there were Thawman's bad business investments. Those turned out to be a lifesaver."

Rhodes tucked his thumb in his belt and stuck out his chest.

"Turned out he had sunk a fortune into one of these cryo companies before digging deeper and reconsidering the... *ethical* considerations. Old Thawman may have lost his financial skin, but it ended up savin' his political hide. Made him look like some kinda saint, suffering a loss like that. Only defense better woulda been if he'd unplugged his dear momma with all them others."

Mick and the governor laughed again. Donald didn't see what was so funny.

"All right, now, you boys take care. The good state of Oklahoma'll have another load for ya in a few weeks."

"Sounds good," Mick said, grasping and pumping that huge Midwestern paw.

Donald shook the governor's hand as well, and then they left him and trudged through the freshly turned soil of the construction site on the way toward their rental. Overhead, against the bright blue Southern sky, contrails like stretched ropes of white yarn revealed the flight-lines of the numerous jets departing the busy hub of Atlanta International. And as the clank and grumble of the construction site faded, the chants from the anti-nuke protestors could be heard outside the tall mesh of security fences beyond.

"Hey, you mind if I drop you off at the airport a little early?" Donald asked, looking up at the streaks of white. They passed through the security gate and into the parking lot, the guard waving them along. "It'd be nice to get a jump on traffic and get down to Savannah with some daylight."

"That's right," Mick said with a grin, "you've got a hot date tonight."

Donald laughed.

"Sure, man. Abandon me and go have a good time with your wife."

"Thanks."

Mick fished out the keys to the rental. "But you know, I was really hoping you'd invite me to come along. I could join you two for dinner, crash at your place, go hit some bars like old times."

"Not a chance," Donald said.

Mick slapped the back of his neck and squeezed. "Yeah, well, happy anniversary anyway."

Donald winced as his friend pinched his neck. "Thanks," he said. "I'll be sure to give Helen your regards."

# 10
2110 • Silo 1

Troy enjoyed a hand of solitaire while Silo 12 collapsed. There was something about the game that he found blissfully numbing. It held off the waves of depression even better than the pills did, the repetition and the complete lack of skill pushing it beyond distraction and into the realm of complete mindlessness.

If a card played, one simply played it. If it didn't: draw another. The truth was, the player won or lost the very moment the computer shuffled the deck. The rest was simply a lengthy process of finding out.

For a computer game, it was absurdly low-tech. It had likely been coded by a bored predecessor with rudimentary programming skills. Instead of graphical cards, there was just a grid of letters and numbers with an asterisk, ampersand, percent, or plus sign to designate the suit. It bothered Troy not to know which symbol stood for hearts or clubs or diamonds. Even though it was arbitrary, even though it didn't really matter, it bugged him to not know.

He had stumbled upon the game by accident while digging through some folders. It took a bit of experimenting to learn how to flip the draw deck with the spacebar and place the cards with the arrow keys, but he had plenty of time to work things like this out. Besides meeting with department heads, going over Merriman's notes, and refreshing himself on the Order, all he had was time. Time to collapse in his office bathroom and cry until snot ran down his chin, time to sit under a scalding shower and shiver, time to hide pills in his cheek and squirrel them away for when the hurt was the worst, time to wonder why the drugs weren't working like they used to, even when he doubled the dosage on his own.

Perhaps the game's numbing powers were why it existed at all, why someone had spent the effort to create it, and why subsequent heads had kept it hidden away. He had seen it on Merriman's face during that elevator ride at the end of his shift. The chemicals only cut through the worst of the pain, that undefinable ache, some grave injury none of them could remember. But lesser wounds resurfaced. The bouts of sudden sadness had to be coming from *somewhere*.

The last few cards fell into place while his mind wandered. The computer had shuffled for a win, and Troy got all the credit for verifying it. The screen flashed *Good Job!* in large block letters, the color morphing in a mesmerizing and psychedelic pattern. It was strangely satisfying to be told this by a homemade game—told that he had done a good job. There was a sense of completion, of having *done* something with his day.

He left the message flashing and glanced around his office for something else to do. There were amendments to be made in the Order, announcements to write up for the Heads of the other silos, and he needed to make sure the vocabulary in these memos abided the ever-changing standards.

He messed up himself, often calling them bunkers instead of silos. It was difficult for those who had lived in the time of the Legacy. An old vocabulary, a way of seeing the world, persisted despite the medication. He felt envious of the others, those who were born and who would die in their own little worlds, who would fall in and out of love, who would keep their hurts in memory, feel them, learn from them, be changed by them. He was jealous of these people even more than he envied the women of his silo who remained in their long-sleep lifeboats—

He stopped himself from going there. The drugs helped. Instead of rushing to the bathroom to cry, he started a new game, a new shuffle, and began flipping through the deck. At times, his hand shook and he had to switch to the other. He remembered something the doctor had said, but that doctor was already gone. Troy didn't feel like meeting the new doctor. Not yet.

There was a dull patch on the spacebar under his thumb, a place where the luster of the plastic had been worn away. Troy wondered how many shifts ago the game had been made. How many thumbs had ticked away the time, *click, click, click*? Then he had a sinister thought: maybe none of his predecessors had come up with the game at all, but it had always been there, planted by the shrinks who knew the numbing effect it would have.

There was a knock on his open door. Troy looked up and saw Randall, who worked across the hall in the psych office, standing in the doorway. Troy waved him inside with one hand and minimized the game with the other. He fidgeted with the copy of the Order on his desk, trying to look busy, which is what he suspected everyone else was doing.

"I've got that beliefs report you wanted." Randall waved a folder.

"Oh, good. Good," Troy took the folder. Always with the folders. He was reminded of the two groups that had built that place: the politicians and the doctors. Both were stuck in a prior era, a time of paperwork. Or it was possible that neither group trusted any data they couldn't shred or burn?

"The head of Silo 6 has a new replacement picked out and processed. He wants to schedule a talk with you, make the induction formal."

"Oh. Okay." Troy flipped through the folder and saw typed transcripts from the communication room about each of the silos. He looked forward to another induction ceremony. Anything he had already done once before filled him with less dread. When he knew the process, the algorithm, all he had to do was reshuffle and flip through the cards. He preferred to avoid the new things and spend more time with the old.

"Also, the population report on Silo 32 is a little troubling." Randall came around his desk. He licked his thumb before sorting through the reports, and Troy glanced at his monitor to make sure he'd minimized the game. "They're getting close to the maximum and fast. Doc Haines thinks it might be a bad batch of birth control implants. The Head of 32, a Biggers, here we go—" Randall pulled out the report. "He denies this, says no one with an active implant has gotten pregnant. He thinks the lottery is being gamed or that there's something wrong with our computers."

"Hmm." Troy took the report and looked it over. Silo 32 had crept above nine thousand inhabitants, and the median age had fallen into the low twenties. "Let's set up a call for first thing in the morning. I don't buy the lottery being gamed. They shouldn't even be running the lottery, right? Until they have more space?"

"That's what I said."

"And all the population accounts for every silo are run from the same computer." Troy tried to not make this sound like a question, but it was. He couldn't remember.

"Yup," Randall said, bailing him out.

"Which means we're being lied to. I mean, this doesn't happen overnight, right? Biggers had to see this coming, which means he knew about it earlier, so either he's complicit, or he's lost control over there."

"Exactly."

"Okay. What do we know about Biggers's second?"

"His shadow?" Randall hesitated. "I'd have to pull that file, but I know he's been in place for a while. Before our shifts."

"Good. I'll speak with him tomorrow. Alone."

"You think we should replace Biggers?"

Troy nodded grimly. The Order was clear on problems that defied explanation: *Start at the top. Assume the explanation was a lie.* Because of the rules, the recipe book, he and Randall were talking about a man being put out of commission as if he were busted machinery or a batch of cookies that didn't come out right.

"Okay, one more thing—"

The thunder of boots down the hallway interrupted the thought. Randall and Troy looked up as Saul bolted into the room, his eyes wide with fear.

"Sirs—"

"Saul. What's going on?"

The communications officer looked like he'd seen a thousand ghosts.

"We need you in the comm room, sir. Right now."

Troy pushed away from his desk. Randall was right behind him.

"What is it?" Troy asked.

Saul hurried down the hallway. "It's Silo 12, sir."

The three of them ran past a man on a ladder who was replacing a long light bulb that had gone dim, the large rectangular plastic cover above him hanging open like a doorway to the heavens. The mechanic watched them race by, an expression on his face like *what's the hurry*?

Troy found himself breathing hard as he struggled to keep up. His fingers were tingling, his toes numb.

"What *about* Silo 12?" he huffed.

Saul flashed a look over his shoulder, his face screwed up with worry. "I think we're losing it, sir."

"What, like contact? You can't reach them?"

"No. Losing *it*, sir. The *silo*. The whole damn thing."

# 11
2049 • Savannah, Georgia

Donald wasn't one for napkins, but he obeyed decorum by shaking the folded cloth loose and draping it in his lap. Each of the napkins at the other settings around the table had been bent into a decorative pyramid that stood upright amid the silverware. He didn't remember the Corner Diner having cloth napkins when he was in high school. Didn't they used to have those paper napkin dispensers that were all dented up from years of abuse? And those little salt and pepper shakers with the silver caps, even those had gotten fancier. A dish of what he assumed was sea salt sat near the flower arrangement, and if you wanted pepper, you had to wait for someone to come around and crack it on your food for you, a service Donald refused to view as an upgrade.

He started to mention this to his wife, thinking Helen would find it funny, and saw that she was still gazing wistfully past him at the other booth. Donald turned in his seat, the original vinyl that had survived outdatedness and moved all the way back around to chic squeaking beneath him. He glanced over at the older couple sitting in the booth where he and Helen had sat on their first date.

"I swear I asked them to reserve it for us," Donald said.

His wife's gaze drifted back to him.

"I think they might've gotten confused when I described which one it was." He stirred the air with his finger. "Or maybe I got turned around when I was on the phone."

She waved her hand. "Sweetie, forget about it. We could be eating grilled cheese at home and I'd be thrilled. I was just staring off into space."

Helen unfolded her own napkin with the delicate care Donald admired her for. It was almost as if she were studying the folds, seeing how to piece it back together, how to return a disassembled thing to its original state. The waiter came over in a bustle and filled their glasses with water, careless drips spotting the white tablecloth. He apologized for the wait, and then left them to wait some more.

"This place sure has changed," he said. He glanced at the menu and would've had a stronger reaction to the prices had D.C. not inoculated him against dollar signs.

"Yeah. It's more grown up," his wife said.

They both reached for their waters at the same time. Donald smiled and held his glass up. "Fifteen years to the day that your father made the mistake of extending your curfew."

Helen smiled. She tapped her glass against his, the ring of expensive crystal sonorous and pretty. "To fifteen more," she said.

They took sips.

"Hell, in another fifteen years, if this place keeps up, we won't be able to *afford* to eat here anymore."

Helen laughed. Donald could imagine the crystal blushing at the sound. She almost hadn't changed a bit since that first date. She was like the Senator that way, ageless but without the medical assistance. Or maybe it was because the changes were so subtle. It wasn't like coming to a restaurant every five years and seeing the leaps all at once. It was how siblings aged rather than distant cousins.

"What're you thinking about?" she asked him.

Donald set down his glass. "Just how beautiful you are."

"If it's work on your mind, I understand."

"No, really, I was sitting here thinking of how unbelievably gorgeous you look tonight."

He tried to catch their waiter's attention, but the aproned man didn't even glance their way as he weaved between the crowded and noisy tables.

"You fly back in the morning?"

"Yeah, but to Boston. I have a meeting with the Senator. Hey, were you thinking of a glass or do you wanna split a bottle?" He looked up from the wine list.

"Let's stick with a glass. I'm still not comfortable letting the car drive at night. You heard about Wendy, right?"

"Yeah, but I heard *she* was the one driving."

Helen frowned. "She told me it was the car. And why are you meeting in Boston?"

He waved his hand. "He's having one of those nano treatments of his. I think he stays locked up in there for a week or so at a time. He still somehow gets his work done—"

"Yeah, by having his minions go out of *their* way—"

"We're not his minions," Donald said, laughing.

"—to come kiss his ring and leave gifts of myrrh."

"C'mon, it's not like that."

She laughed. "I'm only kidding. I just worry that you're pushing yourself too hard. How much of your free time are you spending on this project of his?"

*A lot*, he wanted to say. He wanted to tell his wife how much time he was devoting to this, how grueling the hours were, but he knew what she would say. And so he protected the Senator and said, "It's not as time-consuming as you'd think."

He sipped his water, wishing he had someone to vent to.

"Really? Because it seems like it's the only thing I hear you talking about. I don't even know what else it is you do."

Their waiter came by with a platter full of drinks and said it would just be a moment longer. Helen studied the menu.

"I'll be done with my portion of the plans in another few months," he told her. "And then I won't bore you with it anymore."

"Honey, you don't bore me. I just don't want him taking advantage of you. This isn't what you signed up for. You decided *not* to become an architect, remember? Otherwise, you could've stayed home."

Her gaze drifted over his shoulder again; Donald turned to see if the booth had emptied. He and Helen hadn't even ordered their drinks yet—surely it wouldn't be too late to ask if they could move. But the older couple was still sitting there, eating their food, eyes down on their plates. Maybe they'd been together so long they no longer needed to talk to one another.

"Baby, I want you to know—" He turned back around. "This project we're working on is—"

"It's really important, I know. You've told me, and I believe you. And then in your moments of crippling self-doubt, you admit that your part in the entire scheme of things is superfluous anyway and will never be used."

Donald forgot they'd had that conversation.

"I'll just be glad when it's done," she said. "They can truck the fuel rods through our *neighborhood* for all I care. Just bury the whole thing and smooth the dirt over and stop talking about it."

This was something else. Donald thought about the phone calls and emails he'd been getting from the district, all the headlines and fear mongering over the route the spent rods would take from the port as the trucks skirted Atlanta. Every time Helen heard a peep about the project, all she could likely think of was him wasting his time on it rather than doing his real job. Or the fact that he could've stayed in Savannah and done the same work. But wasn't this all a part of his elected duties? It had all begun to blend together.

Helen cleared her throat. "So—" She seemed to hesitate. "Was Anna at the job site today?"

She peered over the lip of her sweating glass, and Donald realized, in that moment, what his wife was *really* thinking when the CAD-FAC project and the fuel rods came up. It was the insecurity of him working with *her*, of being so far away from home. And he completely understood and sympathized with his wife's discomfort.

"No." He shook his head. "No, we don't really see each other. We send plans back and forth. Mick and I went, just the two of us. He's coordinating a lot of the materials and crews—"

The waiter arrived and pulled his black folio from his apron, clicked his pen. "Can I start you off with drinks?"

Donald ordered two glasses of the house Merlot. Helen declined the offer of an appetizer.

"Every time I bring her up," she said, once their waiter had angled off toward the bar, "you mention Mick. It's like you're trying to change the subject."

"Can we not talk about her?" Donald folded his hands together on the table. "I've seen her once since we started working on this. I set it up so that we didn't have to meet, because I knew you wouldn't approve. I have zero feelings for her, honey. Zilch. Please. This is our night."

"Is working with her giving you second thoughts?"

"Second thoughts about what? About taking on this job? Or about being an architect?"

"About...*anything*." She glanced at the other booth, the booth he should've reserved.

"No. God, no. Honey, why would you even say something like that?"

The waiter came back with their wine. He flipped open his black notebook and eyed the two of them. "Have we decided?"

Helen opened her menu and looked from the waiter to Donald. "I'm going to get my usual," she said. She pointed to what had once been a simple grilled cheese sandwich with fries and what now involved fried green heirloom tomatoes, Gruyère cheese, a honeymaple glaze, and string frites with tartar.

"And for you, sir?"

Donald allowed his eyes to roam the menu. The conversation had him flustered, but he felt the pressure to choose and to choose swiftly.

"I think I'm going to try something different," he said, picking his words poorly.

# 12
2110 • Silo 1

**S**ilo 12 was collapsing, and by the time Troy and the others arrived, the communication room was awash in overlapping radio chatter and the smell of sweat. Four men crowded around a comm station normally manned by a single operator. The men looked precisely how Troy felt: panicked, out of their depth, ready to curl up and hide somewhere. And for whatever reason, it had a calming effect on him. Their panic was his strength. He could fake this. He could hold it together.

Two of the men wore sleepshirts, suggesting that the late shift had been woken up and called in. Troy wondered how long Silo 12 had been in trouble before they finally came and got *him*.

"What's the latest?" Saul asked an older gentleman who was holding a headphone cupped to one ear.

The gentleman turned, his bald head shining in the overhead light, sweat in the wrinkles of his brow, his white eyebrows high with concern. "I can't get anyone to answer the server," he said.

"Give us *just* the feeds from 12," Troy said, pointing to one of the other three workers. A man he had met just a week or so ago pulled off his headset and flipped a switch. The speakers in the room buzzed with overlapping shouts and orders. The others stopped what they were doing and listened.

One of the other men, in his thirties—Troy recognized him from the cafeteria—cycled through dozens of video feeds. It was a chromatic channel-surf of chaos. There was a shot of a spiral staircase crammed with people pushing and shoving. A head disappeared, someone falling down, presumably being trampled as the rest moved on. Across the crowd, eyes were wide in fear, jaws clenched or shouting.

"Let's see the server room," Troy said.

The man at the controls typed something on his keypad. The crush of people disappeared and was replaced with a still view of quiet cabinets, each machine standing upright, the crystal-like precision and rigidity of the layout slightly warped by the wide angle of the lens. The server casings and the grating on the floor throbbed from the blinking overhead lights of an unanswered call.

"What happened?" Troy asked. He felt unusually calm. He was less nervous now with a disaster unfolding than he had been moments ago losing at solitaire.

"Still trying to determine that, sir."

A folder was pressed into his hands. A handful of people gathered in the hallway, peering in. News was spreading, a crowd gathering. Troy felt a trickle of sweat run down the back of his neck, but still that eerie calmness, that resignation to this statistical inevitability.

A desperate voice from one of the radios cut through the rest, the panic palpable:

*"—they're coming through. Dammit, they're bashing down the door. They're gonna get through—"*

Everyone in the comm room seemed to hold their breath, all the jitters and activity ceasing as they listened and waited. Troy was pretty sure he knew which door the panicked man was talking about. It should have been made stronger. A lot of things should have been made stronger.

*"—I'm on my own up here, guys. They're gonna get through. Holy shit, they're gonna get through—"*

"Is that a deputy?" Troy asked. He flipped through the folder. There were status updates from the IT Head of Silo 12. No alarms. Two years since the last cleaning. The fear index was pegged at an eight the last time it had been measured. A little high, but thankfully not too low.

"Yeah, I think that's a deputy," Saul said.

The man at the video feed looked back over his shoulder. "Sir, we're gonna have a mass exodus."

"Their radios are locked down, right?"

Saul nodded. "We shut down the repeater. They can talk amongst themselves, and that's it."

Troy fought the urge to turn and meet the curious faces peering in from the hallway. "Good," he said. The calm was eerie. The priority in this situation was to contain the outbreak: don't let it spread to neighboring cells. This was a cancer. Excise it. Cut the tumor free. Don't mourn the loss. It was just meat. It wasn't the whole body.

The radio crackled:

*"—they're almost in, they're almost in, they're almost in—"*

Troy tried to imagine the stampede, the crush of people, how the panic had spread. He remembered waking up in that god-awful cryopod some months ago, remembered the cold in his bones, the long nightmare still trapped behind the lids of his eyes. The Order was clear on not intervening, but his conscience was muddled. He held out a hand toward the radioman.

"Let me speak to him," Troy said.

Heads swiveled his way. A crowd that thrived on protocol sat stunned. After a pause, the receiver was pressed into his palm. Troy didn't hesitate. He squeezed the mic.

"Deputy?"

*"Hello? Sheriff?"*

The man with the bald and perspiring head cycled through video feeds, then waved his hand and pointed to one of the monitors. The floor number "72" sat in the corner of the screen, and a man in silver coveralls lay slumped over a desk. There was a gun in his hand, a spread of blood around a keyboard.

"That's him?" Troy asked.

The video operator wiped his forehead and nodded.

*"Sheriff? What do I do?"*

Troy clicked the mic. "The sheriff is dead," he told the deputy, surprised by the steadiness of his own voice. He held the transmit button and pondered this stranger's fate. It dawned on him that most of these people thought they were alone in the universe. They had no idea about each other, about their true purpose, and Troy was a god staring down at an anthill. There was another colony a pace away, but the two would never cross. And now he had made contact, a voice from the clouds.

One of the video feeds clicked over to a man holding a handset, the cord spiraling to a radio mounted on the wall. The floor number in the corner read: "1." Troy's connection to this deputy became even more real.

"You need to lock yourself in the holding cell," Troy radioed, seeing that the least obvious solution was the best. It was a temporary solution, at least. "Make sure you have every set of keys."

He watched the man on the video screen.

The entire room, and those in the hallway, watched the man on the video screen.

The door to the upper security office was just visible in the warped bubble of the camera's view. The edges of the door bulged outward because of the lens. The center of the door bulged *inward* because of the mob outside. They were beating the door down. The deputy didn't respond. He dropped the microphone and hurried around the desk. His hands shook so violently as he reached for the keys that the grainy camera was able to pick it up.

The door cracked along the center. Someone in the comm room drew in an audible breath of air. Troy wanted to launch into the statistics. He wanted to explain the cancer analogy. He had studied and trained to be on the *other* end of this, to lead a small group of people in the event of a catastrophe, not to lead them *all*.

Maybe that's why he was so calm. He was watching a horror that he should have been in the middle of, that he should have lived and died through.

The deputy finally secured the keys. He ran across the room and out of sight. Troy imagined him fumbling with the lock on the cell as the door burst in, an angry mob forcing their way through the splintered gap in the wood. It was a solid door, strong, but not strong enough. It was impossible to tell if the deputy had made it to safety. Not that it mattered. It was temporary. It was all temporary. If they opened the doors, if they made it out, the deputy would suffer a fate far worse than being trampled.

"The inner airlock door is open, sir."

Troy nodded. The cancer had probably metastasized in IT, had spread from there. Maybe the Head—but more likely his shadow. Someone with override codes. Here was the curse: a person had to be in charge, had to guard the secrets. Some wouldn't be able to. It was statistically predictable. He reminded himself that it was inevitable, the cards already shuffled, the game just waiting to play out.

"Sir, we've got a breach. The outer door, sir."

"Fire the canisters now," Troy said.

Saul radioed the control room down the hall and relayed the message. The view of the airlock filled with a white fog.

"Secure the server room," Troy added. "Lock it down."

He had this portion of the Order memorized.

"Make sure we have a recent backup just in case. And put them on our power."

"Yessir."

Those in the room who had something to do seemed less anxious than the others, who were left shifting about nervously while they watched and listened.

"Where's my outside view?" Troy asked.

The mist-filled scene of people pushing on each other's backs through a white cloud was replaced with an expansive shot of the outside, of a claustrophobic crowd scampering across a dry land, of people collapsing to their knees, clawing at their faces and their throats, a billowing fog rising up from the teeming ramp.

No one moved or said a word in the comm room. There was a soft cry from the hallway. Troy shouldn't have allowed them to stay and watch. What was the point?

"Okay," he said. "Shut it down."

The overweight man shimmering with sweat fumbled with his keypad. Someone coughed into their fist. The view of the outside went black. There was no point in watching the crowd fight their way back in, no reason to witness the hills while they were coated in those who managed to make it that far.

"I want to know why it happened." Troy turned and studied those in the room. "I want to know, and I want to know what we do to prevent this next time." He handed the folder and the microphone back to the men at their stations. "Don't tell the other silo Heads just yet. Not until we have answers for the questions they'll have."

Saul raised his hand. "What about the people in 12?"

"The only difference between the people in Silo 12 and the people in Silo 13 is that there won't be future generations growing up in Silo 12. That's it. Everyone in all the silos will eventually die. We all die, Saul. Even us. Today was just their day." He nodded to the dark monitor and tried not to picture what was really going on over there. "We knew this would happen, and it won't be the last. Let's concentrate on the others. Learn from it."

There were nods. Saul wiped his brow, then the seat of his pants.

"Individual reports by the end of this shift," Troy said, feeling for the first time that he was actually in charge of something. "And if anyone from 12's IT staff can be raised, debrief them as much as you can. I want to know who, why, and how."

Several of the exhausted people in the room stiffened before trying to look busy. The gathering in the hallway shrank back as they realized the show was over and the boss was heading their way.

The boss.

Troy felt the fullness of his position for the first time, the heavy weight of responsibility. There were murmurs and sidelong glances as he headed back toward his office. There were nods of sympathy and approval, men thankful that they occupied lower posts. Troy strode past them all. He turned the corner, dodging the man on the ladder, who had moved a few fixtures down to replace another bulb.

*More will go out*, Troy thought. For all their careful engineering, there was no way to make a thing infallible. The best they could do is plan ahead, stockpile spares, not mourn the dark and lifeless cylinder as it was discarded and others were turned to with hope.

Back in his office, he closed the door and leaned back against it for a moment. His shoulders stuck to his coveralls with the light sweat worked up from the swift walk. He took a few deep breaths before crossing to his desk and resting his hand on his copy of the Order. The fear persisted that they'd gotten it all wrong. How could a room full of doctors plan for everything? Would it really get easier as the generations went along, as people forgot and the mad whispers from the original survivors faded?

Troy wasn't so sure. He looked over at his wall of schematics, that large blueprint showing all the silos spread out amid the hills, fifty circles spaced out like stars on an old flag he had once served. It was an underground metropolis of sunken skyscrapers, of people completely cut off from each other and the barren world.

A powerful shiver coursed through Troy's body: his shoulders, elbows, and hands twitched. He gripped the edge of his desk until it passed. Opening the top drawer, he fished through his pens until he found a red marker. He crossed to the large schematic, the shivers still wracking his chest.

Before he could consider the permanence of what he was about to do, before he could consider that this mark of his would be on display for every future shift, left to glare down at those who manned this rudderless desk, before he could consider that this may become a trend, an act taken by the other silo Heads, a shared mark of their collective failure, he drew a bold 'X' through Silo 12.

The marker squealed as it was dragged violently across the paper. It seemed to cry out with a distant and mournful voice.

Troy blinked away the blurry vision of the red cross and sagged to his knees. He bent forward until his forehead was against the tall spread of papers, old plans rustling and crinkling as his chest shook, not with shivers, but with sobs.

With his hands in his lap, shoulders bent with the weight of another job he'd been pressured into, the pills shrinking away from the force of his sadness, Troy cried. He bawled as silently as he could so those across the hall wouldn't hear.

In one fist, he clutched the cap from the red marker. In the other, the marker itself, uncovered, tip pressed into his damp palm, spread a stain across his flesh the color of blood.

# 13
## 2049 • RYT Hospital, Dwayne Medical Center

Donald had toured the Pentagon once, had been to the White House twice, went in and out of the Capitol Building a dozen times a week, but nothing he'd seen in D.C. prepared him for the security around RYT's Dwayne Medical Center. The process hardly made the hour-long meeting with the Senator seem worthwhile.

By the time he passed through the full body scanners leading into the nanobiotech wing, he'd been stripped, given a pair of green medical scrubs to wear, had a blood sample taken, and had allowed every sort of scanner and bright light to probe his eyes and record—so they said—the infrared capillary pattern of his face.

Heavy doors and sturdy men blocked every corridor as they made their way deeper and deeper into the NBT wing. When Donald spotted the Secret Service agents—who had been allowed to keep their dark suits and shades, he saw—he knew he was getting close. A nurse scanned him through a final set of double stainless steel doors. The nanobiotic chamber awaited him inside.

Donald eyed the massive machine warily. He'd only ever seen them on TV dramas, and this one loomed even larger in person. It looked like a small submarine that had been marooned on the upper floors of the RYT, or maybe some kind of time machine from a sci-fi flick. Hoses and wires led away from the curved and flawless white exterior in bundles. Studded along the length were several small glass windows that brought to mind the portholes of a ship.

"And you're sure it's safe for me to go in?" He turned to the nurse. "Because I can always wait and visit him later."

The nurse smiled. She couldn't be out of her twenties, had her brown hair wrapped in a knot on the back of her head, was very pretty. "It's perfectly safe," she assured him. "His nanos won't interact with your body. We often treat multiple patients in a single chamber."

She led him to the end of the machine, which Donald thought was shaped like a Tylenol capsule. He could imagine a giant bursting its fist through the wall, plucking the chamber up, and popping it in his mouth. There was a locking wheel on the very end of this massive pill. The nurse gave it a spin, and a hatch opened with a sticky, ripping sound from the rubber seals and a slight gasp of air from the difference in pressure.

"If it's so safe, then why is that thing so *thick*?"

A soft laugh. "You'll be fine." She waved him toward the hatch. "There'll be a slight delay and a little buzz after I seal this door, and then the inner one will unlock. Just spin the wheel and push to open."

"I'm a little claustrophobic," Donald admitted.

God, listen to himself. He was an adult. Why couldn't he just say he didn't want to go in and have that be enough? Why was he allowing himself to be pressured into this?

"Just step inside please, Mr. Keene."

A Secret Service agent in the corner smiled. Donald wanted to ask him why *he* didn't step inside as well if he was so brave.

The nurse placed her hand on the small of Donald's back. Somehow, the pressure of a young and pretty woman watching, not to mention the asshole in the corner, was stronger than his abject terror of the oversized lozenge packed with its invisible machines. He wilted and found himself ducking through the small hatch, his throat constricting with panic.

Why didn't they give him a mask? They should've given him a mask. Or would the nanos pass right through it? How small *were* they? He tried to remember how many zeros in a nanometer as the door behind him thumped shut, leaving him in a small curved space hardly big enough for two. The locks behind him clanked into the jamb. There were tiny silver benches set into the arching walls on either side of him. He tried to stand up, but his head brushed the ceiling. Donald reached for the handle on the inner door, torn between seeking the larger space inside the pill and his fear of the tiny machines that awaited him there.

An angry hum filled the chamber—the hair on the back of his neck stood on end. The air around Donald felt charged with electricity. He wondered if it was to kill any strays. He looked for a speaker, some way to communicate with the Senator through the door so he didn't have to go any further. It felt like he couldn't breathe, like he needed to get *out*. There was no wheel on the outer door. Everything had been taken out of his control—

The inner locks clanked. Donald lunged for the door and tried the handle. Holding his breath, he opened the hatch and escaped the small airlock for the larger chamber in the center of the pill.

"Donald!" Senator Thurman looked up from a thick book. He was sprawled out on one of the benches running the length of the long cylinder. A notepad and pen sat on a small table; a plastic tray held the remnants of dinner.

"Hello, sir." He said this with the minimal parting of lips.

"Don't just stand there, get in. You're letting the buggers out."

Against his every impulse, Donald stepped through and pushed the door shut, and Senator Thurman laughed. "You might as well breathe, son. They could crawl right through your skin if they wanted to."

Donald let out his held breath and shivered. If he'd been alone, or with anyone else, he would've performed his *where-did-the-insect-go?* dance, which entailed flapping his arms and stomping around the room until he was sure the creature was no longer on him. It may have been his imagination, but he thought he felt little pinpricks all over his skin, bites like Savannah's no-see-ems on summer days.

"You can't feel 'em," Senator Thurman said. "It's all in your head. They know the difference between you and me."

Donald glanced down and realized he was scratching his arm.

"Have a seat." Thurman gestured to the bench opposite his. He had the same color scrubs on and a few days' growth on his chin. Donald noticed the far end of the capsule opened on a small bathroom, a shower head with a flexible hose clipped to the wall. Thurman swung his bare feet off the bench and grabbed a half-empty bottle of water, took a sip. Donald obeyed and sat down, a nervous sweat tickling his scalp. There were folded blankets and a few pillows stacked up at the end of the bench. He saw how the frames folded open into cots but couldn't imagine being able to sleep in this little coffin.

"You wanted to see me, sir?" He tried to keep his voice from cracking. The air seemed to possess a metallic taste, a hint of the machines on his tongue. He could picture them there with their little legs and claws, roaming about.

"Drink?" The Senator opened a small fridge below the bench and pulled out a bottle of water.

"Thanks." Donald accepted the water but didn't open it, just enjoyed the cool against his palm. "Mick said he filled you in." He wanted to add that this meeting felt unnecessary.

Thurman nodded. "He did. Met with him yesterday. He's a solid boy." The Senator smiled and shook his head. "The irony is, this class we just swore in? Probably the best bunch the Hill has seen in a very long time."

"The irony?" Donald pressed the cool plastic water bottle against his wrist, where his mind was playing tricks on him with imaginary bug bites.

Thurman waved his hand, shooing the question away. "You know what I love about this treatment?"

*Practically living forever*? Donald nearly asked.

"It gives you time to think. A few days in here, nothing with batteries allowed, just a few books to read and something to write on, it really clears your head."

Donald kept his opinions to himself. He didn't want to admit how creeped out the procedure made him feel, how terrifying it was to be in that room right then. He hated hospitals in general, always feared he would catch something. Knowing that tiny machines were coursing through the

Senator's body, picking through his individual cells and making repairs, grossed him out. Supposedly, your urine turned the color of charcoal once all the machines shut down. He wondered if that would be true for him, just sitting there and breathing the same air.

He shivered at the thought.

"Isn't that nice?" Thurman asked. He took in a deep breath and let it out. "That quiet?"

Donald didn't answer. He realized he was holding his breath.

Thurman looked down at the book in his lap, then lifted his eyes and studied Donald for a few breaths.

"Did you know your grandfather taught me how to play golf?"

Donald laughed. "Yeah. I've seen the pictures of you two together." He flashed back to his grandmother flipping through old albums. She had this weird thing about printing the pictures off her computer and stuffing them in books. Said they became more real once they were displayed like that.

"You and your sister have always felt like family to me," the Senator said.

"Well, I appreciate that, sir." Donald cracked the cap on his water and took a sip. The Senator had definitely been locked up too long. He remembered a night as an undergrad when Mick had gotten sloshed and "opened up to him." It was uncomfortable. A small vent in the corner of the pod circulated some air, but it still felt warm in there.

"I want you in on this project," Thurman said. "All the way in."

Donald swallowed. "Sir. I'm fully committed, I promise."

Thurman raised his hand and shook his head. "No, not like—" He dropped his hand to his lap, glanced at the door, then at one of the small portholes of glass. "You know, I used to think you couldn't hide anything anymore. Not in this age. It's all out there, you know?" He waggled his fingers in the air. "Hell, you ran for office and squeezed through that mess. You know what it's like."

Donald nodded. "Yeah, I had a few things I had to own up to."

The Senator cupped his hands into a bowl. "It's like trying to hold water and not letting a single drop through."

Taking another sip from his bottle, Donald nodded.

"A president can't even get a blow job anymore without the world finding out."

Donald's confused squint had Thurman waving at the air. "Before your time. But here's the thing, here's what I've found, both overseas and in Washington. It's the *unimportant* drips that leak through. The peccadilloes. Embarrassments, not life and death stuff. You want to invade a foreign country? Look at D-Day. Hell, look at Pearl Harbor. Or nine-eleven. Not a problem."

"I'm sorry, sir, I don't see what—"

Thurman's hand flew out, his fingers snapping together as he pinched the air. Donald thought for a moment that he meant for him to not interrupt, to keep quiet, but then the Senator leaned forward and held the pinched pads of his fingers for Donald to see, like he had snatched a mosquito.

"Look," he said.

Donald leaned closer, but he still couldn't make anything out. He shook his head. "I don't see, sir—"

"That's right. And you wouldn't see it coming, either. That's what they've been working on, those snakes." His eyes unfocused for a moment, then snapped back to Donald. "You know what Nobel invented?"

The question seemed to come from nowhere. Donald tilted his head in confusion.

"You know, the peace prize guy."

"Um, dynamite?" Donald wondered where this was going, if the Senator had been cooped up too long.

"TNT, right. You ever think that's funny, the man behind a prize for peace coming up with something so destructive?"

"I think it's because it saved so many lives, sir. At first. Weren't they using something worse for a while?"

"That's right. I forget how sharp you are. Nitroglycerine. One shake and off with your arm."

Donald decided Thurman must be on some kind of sedative for the procedure. The old man was rambling.

"You see, you can't make something for good without someone else figuring out all the *bad* it can do."

"Yessir."

Senator Thurman released the invisible pinch and studied the pad of his thumb for a moment. He blew a puff of air across it. "Anything these puppies can stitch, they can *unstitch*."

He peered across the pod at Donald. "You know why we went into Iran the first time? It wasn't about nukes, I'll tell you that. I crawled through every hole that's ever been dug in those dunes over there, and those rats had a bigger prize they were chasing than nukes. You see, they've figured out how to attack us without being *seen*, without having to blow themselves up, and with *zero* repercussions."

Donald was pretty sure he didn't have the clearance to hear any of this.

"Well, the Arabs didn't figure it out for themselves so much as steal what Israel was working on." He smiled at Donald. "So, of course, we had to start playing catch-up."

"I don't understa—"

"These critters in here are programmed for my DNA, Donny. Think about that. Have you ever had your ancestry tested?" He looked Donald up and down like he was surveying a mottled mutt. "What are you, anyway? Scottish?"

"Maybe Irish, sir. I honestly couldn't tell you." He didn't want to admit that it was unimportant to him; it seemed like a topic Thurman was anything but apathetic about.

"Well these buggers can tell. If they ever get them perfected, that is. They could tell you what clan you came from. And that's what those crazy Iranians are working on: a weapon you can't see, that you can't stop, and if it decides you're Jewish, even a *quarter* Jew—" Thurman drew his thumb across his own neck.

"I thought we were wrong about that. We never found any NBs in Iran."

"That's because they self-destructed. *Remotely*. Poof." The old man's eyes widened.

Donald laughed. "You sound like one of those conspiracy theorists—"

Senator Thurman leaned back and rested his head against the wall. "Donny, the conspiracy theorists sound like *us*."

Donald waited for the Senator to laugh. Or smile. It wasn't happening.

"What does this have to do with me?" he asked. "Or our project?" He suspected the answer was: *nothing*.

Thurman closed his eyes, his head still tilted back against the wall behind him. "You know why Florida has such pretty sunrises?"

Donald wanted to throw his water bottle. He wanted to get up, spin in circles, scream, then beat on the door until they hauled him out of there in a straightjacket. Instead, he took a sip of water and spun the cap back on.

Thurman cracked an eye. Seemed to study him. He finally realized Donald wasn't going to guess.

"It's because the sand from Africa blows clear across the Atlantic."

Donald nodded. He saw what the Senator was getting at. He'd heard the same fear mongering on the 24-hour news programs, how toxins and tiny machines can circle the globe, just like seeds and pollens have done for millennia.

"It's coming, Donny. I know it is. I've got eyes and ears everywhere, even in here. I asked you to meet me here because I want you to have a seat at the *after* party."

"Sir?"

"You and Helen both."

Donald scratched his arm and glanced at the door. He wanted out of there.

"It's just a contingency plan for now, you understand? There are plans in place for anything. Mountains for the president to crawl inside of, but we need something else."

Donald remembered the congressman from Atlanta prattling on about zombies and the CDC. This sounded like more of that nonsense.

"I'm happy to serve on any committee you think's important—"

"Good." The Senator took the book from his lap and handed it to Donald, who was prepared this time for how heavy it would be. "Read this," Thurman said.

Donald checked the cover. It was familiar, but instead of French script, it read: *The Order*. He opened it to a random page and started skimming.

"That's your bible from now on, son. When I was in the war, I met boys no higher than your knee who had the entire Qur'an memorized, every stinkin' verse. You need to do better."

"Memorize?"

"As near as you can. And don't worry, you've got a couple of years."

Donald laughed. He snapped the book shut and studied the spine. "Good. I'll need it." He wanted to know if there would be a raise involved or a ton of committee meetings. This sounded ludicrous, but he wasn't about to refuse the old man, not with his reelection coming up every two years.

"All right. Welcome." Thurman leaned forward and held out his hand. Donald tried to get his palm deep into the Senator's. It made the older man's grip hurt a lot less. "You're free to go."

"Thank you, sir."

He stood and exhaled in relief. Cradling the book, he moved to the airlock door.

"Oh, and Donny?"

He turned back. "Yessir?"

"The National Convention in a couple of years. I want you to go ahead and pencil it into your schedule. And make sure Helen is there."

Donald felt goose bumps shiver down his arms. Screw the committee, *this* was what he wanted to hear. A real possibility of promotion. Maybe a speech on the big stage. That was the ticket that moved congressmen from Rayburn to Dirksen and transformed two-year terms to six.

"Absolutely, sir." He knew he was smiling.

"Oh, and I'm afraid I haven't been completely honest with you about the critters in here."

"Sir?" Donald swallowed. His smile melted. He had one hand on the hatch's wheel. His mind resumed playing tricks on him, the taste on his tongue metallic, the pricks everywhere on his skin.

"Some of the buggers in here are very much for you."

Senator Thurman stared at Donald for a breath, and then he started laughing.

Donald turned, sweat dripping from his brow as he worked the wheel in the door. He nearly dropped the book twice, his palms were so sweaty. It wasn't until he secured the airlock, the seals deadening the laughter and the bad joke, that he could breathe again.

The air around him buzzed, a jolt of static to kill any strays. Donald blew out his breath. He exhaled the unseen and imagined torment in his lungs to their electrified death. And then he fought back the tears and the panic, the urge to scream. He didn't want the pretty nurse or the man in the sunglasses to see him cry.

# 14
2110 • Silo 1

The shrinks kept Troy's door locked and delivered his meals while he went through the Silo 12 reports alone. He spread the pages across his keyboard—safely away from the edge of his desk. This way, when stray tears fell, they hit only wood. He routinely palmed them off and smeared them into his thigh.

For some reason, Troy couldn't stop crying. The shrinks with the strict meal plans had taken him off his meds the last two days, long enough to compile his findings sober and free to remember. He had a deadline. After he put his final notes together, they would get him something to cut through the pain.

Images of the dying interfered with his thoughts. It was always that view of the outside, of people suffocating and falling to their knees. Troy remembered giving the order. What he regretted most was making someone else push the button.

Coming off his meds brought back other random haunts. He remembered his father. He remembered events from before his orientation. And it confused him that a billion dead could be an ache in his gut while a few thousand made him want to curl up and die.

Maybe it was because he saw himself as a steward to the thousands. They were in his charge. But then again: hadn't that been true of the billions? Hadn't they all been stewards of each other? Or was inaction somehow a lesser sin? Was keeping quiet less evil than barking orders?

The reports on his keyboard told a story, a predictable story. Troy knew there were paragraphs in The Legacy that told the same tale. What he didn't understand was how something could be predictable without being *preventable*. Statistics were magic like this: they could tell you with near-certainty that a thing would occur, without a hint of when or where.

There was something else about those reports; they reminded him of parts of the Legacy. He thought of men like Hitler, Stalin, and Napoleon. All it took was a lot of seemingly decent people to put the wrong person in power and then fall under their spell.

Troy's stomach grumbled; it was an impatient fist opening and closing, asking for the pill. He wiped his forehead with his sleeve, which was already dark and damp with his discomfort. That wasn't right, blaming it on one person. Was it? He glanced around his office and wished there was a copy of the Legacy he could consult. But the books were across the hall, and his door was locked. He tried to remember on his own, but the past was fuzzy. The past was more distant than minds were meant for.

The report in his hand told a story, a story of a shadow who had lost his nerve, an IT Head who couldn't see the dark thing spreading out at her feet, and an honest enough Security chief who had chosen poorly.

The keycodes for each video feed sat in the margins. Again, it reminded him of another old book; the references had a similar style:

*Jason 2:17* brought up a slice of the shadow's feed. Troy followed the action on his monitor. A young man, probably in his late teens or early twenties, sat on a server room floor. His back was to the camera, the corners of a plastic tray visible in his lap. He was bent over a meal, the bony knots of his spine casting dots of shadow down the back of his coveralls.

Troy watched. He glanced at the report to check the timecode. He didn't want to miss it.

In the video, Jason's right elbow worked back and forth. It was easy to imagine him eating, perhaps sawing into a delicious cut of pork. The moment was coming. Troy willed himself to not blink, could feel tears coat his eyes from the effort.

A noise startled Jason. The young IT shadow glanced to the side, his profile visible for a moment. He grabbed the tray from his lap; it was the first time Troy could spot the rolled-up sleeve. And there, as he fought with the cuff to roll it back down, were the dark parallel lines across his forearm, and nothing on his tray that called for a knife.

The rest of the clip was of Jason speaking to the IT Head, her demeanor motherly and tender, a touch on his shoulder, a squeeze of his elbow. Troy could imagine her voice. He had spoken to her once or twice to take down a report. In a few more weeks, they would've scheduled a time to speak with Jason and induct him formally.

The clip ended with Jason descending back into the hole, a shadow swallowing a shadow. The Head of IT—the *true* Head of Silo 12—stood alone for a moment, hand on her chin. She looked so *alive*. Troy had a childlike impulse to reach out and brush his fingers across the monitor, to acknowledge this ghost, to apologize for letting her down.

Instead, he saw something the reports missed. He watched her body twitch toward the hatch, stop, freeze for a moment, then turn away.

Troy clicked the slider at the bottom of the video to see it again. Jason popped on the screen as he went back too far. There she was rubbing his shoulder, talking to him, Jason nodding. She squeezed his elbow, was concerned about him. Jason was assuring her everything was fine. He was great. Thanks for the concern.

Once he was gone, once she was alone, the mental machinations began. Troy couldn't know it, but he could *sense* it. She had her doubts. Here was her chance to destroy the dark thing she'd helped create, a twitch in that direction, reconsidering, turning away.

Troy paused the video and made some notes, jotted down the times. The shrinks would have to verify his findings. Shuffling the papers, he wondered if there was anything he needed to see again. Here was a story like in that old collection of books with human names, the chapters in hours, verses in minutes. It was the fall of Jericho, the legend of Gomorrah. A black shadow had fallen upon Silo 12. A decent woman had been murdered because she could not bring herself to do the same, to kill in order to protect. And a Security chief had let loose a monster who had mastered the art of concealing his pain, a young man who had learned how to manipulate others, who wanted *out*.

He typed up his conclusions. It was a dangerous age for shadowing, he noted in his report. Here was a boy crossing that dire Rubicon between his teens and twenties, those years when healthy young bucks are studying their herd and looking for signs the Alpha has gone gray. It was an age deep in hormones and shallow in control. Troy asked in his report if anyone in their twenties could ever be ready. He made mention of the first head of IT he had inducted, the question the boy had asked after hearing tales from his demented grandmother. Was it right to expose anyone to these truths? Could men of such fragile age be expected to endure such blows without shattering?

What he didn't add, what he asked himself, was if anyone at *any* age could ever be ready.

There was precedence, he typed, for limiting certain positions of authority by age. And while this would lead to shorter terms due to the simple math of longevity—which meant subjecting more unfortunate souls to the abuse of being locked up and shown their Legacy—wasn't it better to go through a damnable process more often rather than take risks such as these?

He hammered the keyboard as tears related to some unnamable other thing splashed to his desk. He knew this report would matter little. There was no planning for insanity. Enough revolutions and elections, enough transfers of power, and eventually a madman would caress the reins. He would caress the reins and reach for a crop, and instead of steering, he would whip for no other reason than that he *could*.

And so Troy printed his report assuming nothing would come of it. These were the odds they had planned for. This was why they had built so many. He rose from his desk and walked to the door, slapped it soundly with the flat of his palm. In the corner of his office, a printer hummed and shot four pages out of its mouth. Troy took them; they were still warm as he slid them into the folder, these reports on the newly dead and still dying. He could feel the life and warmth draining from those printed pages. Soon, they would be as cool as the air around them.

A key rattled in his lock before the door opened. Troy wiped his cheeks and then his desk. He dragged his palm across the seat of his pants, destroying the evidence.

"Done already?" Victor asked. The gray-haired psychologist stood across from his desk, keys singing as they returned to his pocket. He held a small plastic cup in his hand.

Troy handed him the folder. "The signs were there," he told the doctor, "but they weren't acted upon."

Victor took the folder with one hand and held out the plastic cup with the other. A blue blur of forgetting rattled softly inside.

Troy typed a few commands on his computer and wiped his copy of the videos. The cameras were no good for predicting and preventing these kinds of problems. There were too many to watch all at once. You couldn't get enough people to sit and monitor an entire populace, which meant they were only good for sorting through the wreckage, the aftermath.

"Looks good," Victor said, flipping through the folder. The plastic cup sat on Troy's desk. There were two pills inside. It was like the dosage at the start of his shift, a little extra to cut through the little extra. Looking down at them, he saw that there was still a wet smear across his desk. He wondered if it would turn to salt once the moisture evaporated away.

"Would you like me to fetch you some water?"

Troy shook his head. He hesitated. Looking up from the twin pills, he asked Victor a question.

"How long do you think it'll take? Silo 12, I mean. Before all of those people are gone."

Victor shrugged. "Not long, I imagine. Days."

Troy nodded. Victor watched him carefully. Troy tilted his head back and rattled the pills past trembling lips. There was the bitter taste of forgetting on his tongue, and then he made a show of swallowing.

"I'm sorry that it was your shift," Victor said. "I know this wasn't the job you signed up for."

Troy nodded.

"I'm actually glad it was mine," he said after a moment. "I'd hate for it to have been anyone else's."

Victor rubbed the folder with one hand. "You'll be given a commendation in my report."

"Thank you," Troy said. He didn't know what the fuck for.

With a wave of the folder, Victor finally turned to leave and go back to his desk across the hall where he could sit and glance occasionally up at Troy.

But he had to walk to get there. And in that brief interval, when no one was looking, like a young shadow sawing into his arm because the pain was better than the numb, Troy spat the two blue blurs into the palm of his hand.

Shaking his mouse with one hand, waking up his monitor so he could boot a game of solitaire, Troy smiled across the hallway at Victor, who smiled back. And in his other hand, still sticky from the outer coating dissolved by his saliva, two pills nestled in a palm dyed pink. The blood-red stain from the day before was already beginning to fade. But Troy was tired of fading. He had decided to remember.

# 15
## 2049 • Savannah, Georgia

Donald sped down Highway 17, driving manually, a red light on his dash flashing a warning as he exceeded the local speed limit. He didn't care about being pulled over, didn't care about being wired a ticket or his insurance rates creeping up. It all seemed trivial. The fact that there were circuits riding along in his car keeping track of everything he did paled in comparison to the suspicion that machines in his *blood* were doing the same.

The tires squealed as he spiraled down his exit ramp too fast. He merged onto Berwick Boulevard, the overhead lights strobing through the windshield as he flew beneath them. Glancing down at his lap, he watched the gold inlay text on the book throb with the rhythm of the passing streetlights.

Order. Order. Order.

He had read enough to worry, to wonder what he'd gotten himself mixed up in. Helen had been right to warn him, had been wrong about the scale of the danger.

Turning into their neighborhood, Donald remembered an ancient conversation—he remembered her begging him not to run for office, that it would change him, that he couldn't fix anything up there, but that he could sure as hell come home broken.

How right had she been?

He pulled up to the house and had to leave the car by the curb. Her Jeep was in the middle of the driveway. One more habit formed in his absence, a reminder that he didn't live there anymore, didn't have a real home.

Leaving his bags in the trunk, he took just the book and his keys. It was enough of a load, that book.

The motion light came on as he neared the stoop. He saw a form by the door, heard frantic scratching on the other side. Helen opened the door, and Karma rushed out, tail whacking the side of the jamb, tongue lolling, so much bigger in just the few weeks that he'd been away.

Donald crouched down and rubbed her head, let the dog lick his cheek.

"Good girl," he said. He tried to sound happy. The cool emptiness in his chest intensified from being home, from lying to their dog about his mood. The things that should've felt comforting just made him feel worse.

"Hey, honey." He smiled up at his wife.

"You're early."

Helen wrapped her arms around his neck as he stood. Karma sat down and whined at them, tail swishing on the concrete. Helen's kiss tasted like coffee.

"I took an earlier flight."

He glanced over his shoulder at the dark streets of his neighborhood. As if anyone needed to follow him.

"Where're your bags?"

"I'll get 'em in the morning. C'mon, Karma. Let's go inside." He steered his dog through the door.

"Is everything okay?" Helen asked.

Donald went to the kitchen. He set the book down on the island and fished in the cabinet for a glass. Helen watched him with concern as he pulled a bottle of brandy out of the cabinet.

"Baby. What's going on?"

"Maybe nothing," he said. "Lunatics—" He poured three fingers of brandy, looked to Helen and raised the bottle to see if she wanted any. She shook her head. "Then again," he continued, "maybe there's something to it—" He took more than a sip. His other hand hadn't left the neck of the bottle.

"Baby, you're acting strange. Come sit down. Take off your coat."

He nodded and let her help him remove his jacket. He slid his tie off, saw the worry on her face, knew it was a reflection of his own. He tried to relax the knot he could feel above his nose, the scrunched brow that was frozen on his forehead—it was the emotional and physical antithesis of sore cheeks from smiling too much.

"What would you do if you thought it all might end?" he asked his wife. "What would you do?"

"If what? You mean us? Oh, you mean life. Honey, did someone pass away? Tell me what's going on."

"No, not someone. Everyone. Everything."

He tucked the bottle under his arm, grabbed his drink and the book, and went to the living room. Helen and Karma followed. Karma was already on the sofa waiting for him to plop down before he got there, a goofy smile, oblivious to anything he was saying, just thrilled for the pack to be reunited.

"It sounds like you've had a very long day—" Helen said, trying to find excuses for him.

Donald sat down on the sofa and put the bottle and book on the coffee table. He pulled his drink away from Karma's curious nose.

"I have something I have to tell you," he said.

Helen stood in the middle of the room, her arms crossed. "That'd be a nice change." She smiled to let him know it was meant in jest. Donald nodded.

"I know, I know," he said. His eyes fell to the book, then drifted toward what he figured was the general direction of Atlanta. "This isn't about that project. And honestly, do you think I enjoy keeping my life from you?"

Helen crossed to the recliner next to the sofa and sat down. "What is this about?" she asked.

"I've been told it's okay to tell you about a...promotion. Well, more of an assignment than a promotion. Not an assignment, really, more like being on the National Guard. Just in case—"

Helen reached over and squeezed his knee. "Take it easy," she whispered. Her eyebrows were lowered, confusion and worry lurking in the shadows there.

Donald took a deep breath. He was still revved up from running the conversation over in his head, from driving too fast. The weeks since his meeting with Thurman were a blur, a blur of reading too much into the book and too much into that conversation. He couldn't tell if he was piecing something together or just mentally falling apart.

"How much have you followed what's going on in Iran?" he asked, scratching his arm. "And Korea?"

She shrugged. "I see blurbs online."

"Mmm." He took a burning gulp of liquor, smacked his lips, and tried to relax and enjoy the numbing chill as it traveled through his body. "They're working on ways to take everything out," he said.

"Who? *We* are?" Helen's voice rose. "We're thinking of taking *them* out?"

"No, no—"

"Are you sure I'm allowed to hear this—?"

"No, sweetheart, they're designing weapons to take *us* out. Weapons that can't be stopped, that can't be defended against."

Helen leaned forward, her hands clasped, elbows resting on her knees. "Is this stuff you're learning in Washington? Classified stuff?"

He waved his hand. "Beyond classified. Look, you know why we went into Iran—"

"I know why they *said* we went in—"

"It wasn't bullshit," he said, cutting her off. "Well, maybe it was. Maybe they hadn't figured it out yet, hadn't mastered how—"

"Honey, slow down."

"Yeah." He took another deep breath. He had an image in mind of a large mountain out West, a concrete road disappearing straight into the rock, thick vault doors standing open as files of politicians crowded inside with their families and just a handful of belongings.

"I met with the Senator a few weeks ago." He stared down into the ginger-colored liquor in his glass.

"In Boston," Helen said.

He nodded. "Right. Well, he wants us to be on this alert team—"

"You and Mick."

He turned toward his wife. "No, us."

"*Us?*" Helen placed a hand on her chest. "What do you mean, us? You and me?"

"Now listen—"

"You're volunteering *me* for one of his—?"

"Sweetheart, I had no idea what this was all about." He set his glass on the coffee table and grabbed the book. "He gave me this to read."

Helen frowned at the book. "What is that?"

"It's like an instruction manual for the—well, for the *after*. I think."

Helen got up from the recliner and stepped between him and the coffee table. She nudged Karma out of the way, the dog grunting at being disturbed. Sitting down beside him, she put a hand on his back, her eyes shiny with worry.

"Donny, were you drinking on the plane?"

"No." He pulled away. "Dammit baby, listen to me. It doesn't matter *who* has them, it only matters *when*. Don't you see? This is the ultimate threat. A world-ender. I've been reading about the possibilities on this website—"

"A website," she said, voice flat with skepticism.

"Yeah. Listen. Remember those treatments the Senator takes? These nanos are like synthetic life. Imagine if someone turned them into a virus that didn't care about its host, that didn't need *us* in order to spread. They could be out there already—" He tapped his chest, glanced around the room suspiciously, took a deep breath. "They could be in every one of us right now, little timer circuits waiting for the right moment—"

"Sweetheart—"

"Very bad people are working on this, trying to make this happen." He reached for his glass. "We can't sit back and let them strike first. We can't let them strike first. So we're gonna do it." There were ripples in the liquor. His hand was shaking. "God, baby, I'm pretty sure we're gonna do it before *they* can—"

"You're scaring me, honey—"

"Good." Another burning sip. He held the glass with both hands to keep it steady. "We should be scared."

"Do you want me to call Dr. Martin?"

"Who?" He tried to make room between them, bumped up against the armrest. "Charlotte's doctor? The *shrink*?"

She nodded gravely.

"I need you to listen to me for one second," he said, holding up a finger. "Listen to what I'm telling you. These tiny machines are *real*." He thought about the comparison Thurman had made to Alfred Nobel and TNT, how good inventions could be hijacked and steered in dangerous ways. His mind was racing. It would be easy to babble and convince her of nothing but his insanity.

"Look," he said. "We use them in medicine, right?"

Helen nodded. She was giving him a chance, a slim one. But he could tell she really wanted to go call someone. Her mother, a doctor, *his* mother.

"It's like when we discovered radiation, okay? The first thing we thought was that this would be a cure, a medical discovery. X-rays, and then people were taking drops of radium like an elixir—"

"They poisoned themselves," Helen said, "thinking they were doing something good."

She seemed to relax a little. "Is this what you're worried about?" she asked him. "That the nanos are going to mutate and turn on us? Are you still freaked out from being inside that machine?"

Her worry had turned to sympathy, her fear melting into compassion. Donald remembered the call he'd made after his meeting in the RYT, how he'd been freaking out and acting hysterical from his claustrophobia and an attack of the heebie-jeebies.

"No, nothing like that. I'm talking about how we looked for medicinal uses first, then ended up building the bomb. This is the *same thing*." He paused, hoping she would get it. "I'm starting to think we're building them, too. Tiny machines, just like the ones in the nanobaths that stitch up people's skin and joints, only *these* would tear people down. And they would be able to unstitch *anything*."

Helen didn't react. Didn't say a word. Donald realized he sounded crazy, that every bit of this was already online and in podcasts that radiated out from lonely basements on lonely airwaves. The Senator had been right. Mix truth and lies and you couldn't tell them apart. The book on his coffee table and a zombie survival guide were the same things.

"I'm telling you they're real," he said, unable to stop himself. "They'll be able to reproduce. They'll be invisible. There won't be any warning when they're set loose, just dust in the breeze, okay? Reproducing and reproducing, this invisible war will wage itself all around us while we're turned to mush."

Helen was a statue. She was a pier withstanding the tide. He knew what was happening, could see it from the outside like an observer. She was waiting for him to finish, for him to stop crashing against her, and then she would call her mom and ask what to do. She would call Dr. Martin and get his advice.

Donald started to complain, could feel the anger welling up inside of himself, and knew that anything he said would confirm her fears rather than convince her of his own.

He looked around the room, around the house that was becoming more and more foreign to him. The table beside the front door was different. He hadn't noticed that when he entered.

"Is there anything else?" she whispered. She was looking for permission to leave and make her phone calls, to talk to someone rational.

Donald felt numb. Helpless and alone. He felt like crying but knew that would seal the deal.

"The National Convention is going to be held in Atlanta." He wiped at the bottoms of his eyes, tried to make it look like weariness, like the strain of travel. "The DNC hasn't announced it yet, but I heard from Mick before I got on the flight. The Senator wants us there, is already planning something big."

He turned to Helen, saw that she was blurry, knew his eyes must be shining from holding back the madness. "The Senator wants us both there, okay?"

"Of course, baby." She rested her hand on his thigh, was looking at him like he was her patient, or some kind of invalid.

"And I'm going to ask that I spend more time down here, maybe do some of my work from home on weekends, keep a closer eye on the project."

"That'd be great." She rested a hand on his arm. The concern on her face was of icy calmness, that pier riding out the tide. What he thought he knew seemed to crumble a little; the secrets burning in his blood began to temper. Donald felt himself on the verge of sobbing.

"I want us to be good to each other," he said. "For whatever time we have left—"

"Shhhh, baby, it's okay." She wrapped her arm around his back and shushed him again, trying to soothe him.

"I love you," she said.

He wiped at his eyes.

"We'll get through this," she told him.

Donald bobbed his head. "I know," he said. "I know we will."

The dog grunted and nuzzled her head into Helen's lap, could sense something was wrong. Donald scratched the pup's neck. He looked up at his wife, tears in his eyes. "I know we will," he said again, trying to soothe himself. "But what about everyone *else*?"

# 16
2110 • Silo 1

Troy needed to see a doctor. Ulcers had formed in both sides of his mouth, down between his gums and the insides of his cheeks. He could feel them like little wads of tender cotton embedded in his flesh, little puckers of numbness. Between breakfast and dinner, he alternated. In the morning, he kept the pill tucked down on the left side. For supper, he squirreled it away on the right. On either side, it would burn and dry out his mouth with the bitter bite of the medicine, but he would endure it.

He rarely employed napkins during meals, a bad habit he had formed long ago. They went into his lap to be polite and then went on his plate when he was done. Now he had a different routine. One quick small bite of something, wipe his mouth, spit out the burning blue capsule, take a huge gulp of water, swish it around.

It was a dereliction of duty, he knew. He was the captain of a creaking ship long at sea, and here he was tonguing a loose tooth and refusing to swallow his daily allotment of lime. The scurvy was taking him and he was letting it, even though this placed the others at risk. He knew this and felt bad about it, but he couldn't will himself to do anything else.

The hard part was not checking to see if anyone was watching while he spit it out. He sat with his back to the wallscreen and went through this process while he imagined eyes in white coveralls drilling through the side of his head.

But he didn't look. He chewed his food. He remembered to use his napkin occasionally, to wipe with both hands, always with both hands, pinching across his mouth, staying consistent. He smiled at the man across from him and made sure the pill didn't fall out. The man's gaze drifted over Troy's shoulder as he stared at the view.

Troy didn't turn to look for himself. There was still the same draw, the same compulsion to be as high as possible, to escape the suffocating depths, but he no longer felt any desire to see outside. Something had changed.

He spotted Hal at the next table over—recognized his bald and splotchy scalp. The old man was sitting with his back to Troy. Troy waited to catch his eye, but Hal never turned to look.

He finished his corn and worked on his beets. It had been long enough since spitting out his pill to risk a glance toward the serving line. Tubes spat food; plates rattled on trays; one of the doctors from Victor's office stood beyond the glass serving line, arms crossed, a wan smile on his face. He was scanning the men in line and looking out over the tables. Why? What was there to keep an eye on? Troy wanted to know. He had dozens of burning questions like this; answers sometimes rose toward the surface, but they skittered away if he trained his thoughts on them.

The beets were awful.

He ate the last of them while the gentleman across the table stood with his tray. It wasn't long before someone took his place. Troy looked up and down the row of adjoining tables. The vast majority of the workers sat on the *other* side so they could see out. Only a handful sat like Hal and himself. It was strange that he'd never noticed this before.

In the past weeks, it seemed patterns were becoming easier to spot, even as other faculties slipped and stumbled. He cut into a rubbery hunk of canned ham, his knife screeching against his plate, and wondered when he'd get some real sleep. He couldn't ask the doctors for anything to help, couldn't show them his gums. They might find out he was off his other meds. The insomnia was awful. It was as though his body had grown scared of the dreams that awaited. He might doze off for a minute or two, but deep sleep eluded him. And instead of remembering anything concrete, all he had were these dull aches, these bouts of sadness, the feeling that something was wrong, that he'd known what was going on a week ago, maybe even a month ago, but no further back than that.

He chewed on this thought and his ham both. He caught one of the doctors watching him. Troy looked down the table and saw men shoulder to shoulder on the other side, empty seats lined up across from them. It wasn't long ago that he wanted to sit and stare, mesmerized by the gray hills. And now he felt sick when he caught even a glimpse; the view brought him near to tears. He eyed the corner of the room where he knew a camera was hidden. And Troy had an idea of what they were looking for. They were looking for signs of remembrance.

He stood immediately with his tray, then worried he was being transparent. Obvious. The napkin fell from his lap and landed on the floor, something skittering away from his foot.

Troy's heart skipped a beat. He bent and snatched the napkin, hurried down the line, looking for the pill. He bumped into a chair that had been pulled back from the table, felt all the eyes on him, the sailors watching their captain dance drunkenly across the deck, losing his mind, teeth falling out and clattering away.

The pill. He found it and scooped it up with his napkin, the tray teetering dangerously in his palm. He stood and composed himself, could feel a trickle of sweat itch his scalp and run down the back of his neck. It seemed like half the room had stopped eating to watch him. Everyone knew. Knew he was losing his mind.

He turned and walked toward the water fountain. It took an iron force of will to not glance up at the cameras or over at the doctors. He was losing it, he knew. Growing paranoid. Just a little over a month left on this shift. He could do it.

Trying to walk naturally with so many eyes on him was impossible. He rested the edge of his tray on the water fountain, stepped on the lever with his foot, and topped up his glass. This was why he had gotten up: he was thirsty. He felt like announcing the fact out loud. He wasn't crazy. He was like them. He couldn't remember anything.

Returning to the tables, Troy squeezed between two other workers and sat down facing the screen. He balled up his napkin, felt the blue kernel hidden within its folds, and tucked it between his thighs. A bite of ham remained. He picked up his fork and jabbed it. He sat there, facing the screen, but he didn't dare look.

# 17
2051 • Washington D.C.

The fat raindrops on the canopy outside De'Angelos sounded like rhythmless fingers tapping on a drum. The traffic on L Street hissed through puddles gathering against the curb, and the asphalt that flashed between the cars gleamed shiny and black from the streetlights. Donald shook two pills out of a plastic vial and into his palm. Two years on the meds. Two years completely free of anxiety, gloriously numb.

He glanced at the label and thought of his sister, popped them in his mouth and swallowed. He was sick of the rain, preferred the quiet cleanliness of the snow. But another winter had been too warm for any chance of that.

Keeping out of the foot traffic flowing through the front doors—umbrellas jostling against umbrellas—he cradled his cell phone against his ear and listened patiently while his wife urged Karma to pee.

"Maybe she doesn't need to go," he suggested. He dropped the vial into his coat pocket and cupped his hand over his phone as the lady beside him wrestled with her umbrella, water flicking everywhere.

Helen continued to cajole Karma with a raft of words the poor dog didn't understand. These were their conversations of late. Nothing real to say, disjointed daily routines, babbling about the trivial amid long silences. "But she hasn't been since *lunch*," Helen insisted.

"She didn't go somewhere in the house, did she?"

"She's four years old."

Donald forgot. Lately, time felt locked in a bubble. He wondered if his medication was causing that or if it was the workload. Whenever anything seemed...off anymore, he always assumed it was the medication. Before, it could have been the vagaries of life; it could have been anything. Somehow, it felt worse to have something concrete and new to pin it on.

On the other end of the line, Helen pleaded with the dog. There was shouting across the street. Donald looked up to see two homeless men yelling at each other in the rain, squabbling over a piece of cardboard or a bag of tin cans or some personal offense from the day before. He watched morosely as more umbrellas were shaken and more fancy dresses flowed into the restaurant. Here was a city charged with governing all the others, and it couldn't even take care of itself. These things used to worry him more. He patted the capsule in his jacket pocket, a comforting twitch he'd developed.

"She won't go," his wife said exhaustedly.

"Baby, I'm sorry I'm up here and you have all that to take care of. But look, I really need to get inside. We're trying to wrap up final revisions on these plans tonight—"

"How is everything going with that? Are you almost done?"

A file of taxis drove by, hunting for fares, fat tires rolling across sheets of water like hissing snakes. Donald watched as one of them slowed to a stop, brakes squealing from the wet.

He didn't recognize the man stepping out, coat held up over his head. It wasn't Mick.

"Huh? Oh, it's going great. Yeah, we're basically done, maybe a few tweaks here and there. The outer shells are poured, and the lower floors are in—"

"I meant, are you almost done working with *her*?"

He turned away from the traffic to hear better. "Who, Anna? Yeah. Look, I've told you. We've only consulted here and there. Most of it's done electronically."

"And Mick is there?"

"Yup."

Another cab slowed as it passed by. Donald turned at the sound of squealing brakes, but the car didn't stop.

"Okay. Well, don't work too late. Call me tomorrow."

"I will. I love you."

"Love you—Oh! Good girl! That's a good girl, Karma—!"

"I'll talk to you tomorr—"

But the line was already dead. Donald glanced at his phone before putting it away, shivered once from the cool fall evening and from the moisture in the air. He pressed through the crowd outside the door, fought through patrons studying the rain and calling car services. Inside, he waved off the maître d' and made his way to the table.

"Everything okay?" Anna asked. She sat alone at a table with three settings. A wide-necked sweater had been pulled down to expose one shoulder. She pinched her second glass of wine by its delicate stem, a pink half-moon of lipstick on its rim. Her auburn hair was tied up in a bun, the freckles across her nose almost invisible behind a thin and expert veil of makeup. She looked, impossibly, more alluring than she had in college.

"Yeah, everything's fine." Donald twisted his wedding ring with his thumb—a habit. "Have you heard from Mick?" He reached into his pocket and pulled out his cell, checked his texts. He thought of firing off another one, but there were already four unanswered messages sitting there.

"Nope. Wasn't he flying in from Texas this morning? Maybe his flight was delayed."

She took another sip of wine and studied him over the rim. He saw that his glass, which he'd been nursing, had been topped up while he was gone. Donald knew Helen would disapprove of him sitting there alone with Anna, even though nothing was going to happen. Nothing ever could. It was just the potential, the act of placing himself in danger.

"We could always do this another time," he suggested. "I'd hate for Mick to be left out."

She set down her glass and studied the menu. "Might as well eat while we're here. Be a little late to find something else. Besides, Mick's logistics are independent of our design. We can send him our materials report later."

Donald reluctantly unfolded his napkin and placed it in his lap. Anna leaned to the side and reached for something in her purse, her sweater falling dangerously open. Donald looked away quickly, a flush of heat on the back of his neck. She pulled out her tablet and placed it on top of his manila folder, the screen flashing to life.

"I think the bottom third of the design is solid." She spun the tablet for him to see. "I'd like to sign off on it so they can start layering the next few floors in."

"Well, a lot of these are yours," he said, thinking of all the mechanical spaces at the bottom. "I trust your judgment."

He picked the tablet up, relieved that this was still going to be about work. He felt like a fool for thinking Anna had anything else in mind. They had been exchanging emails and updating each other's plans for over two years. There was never a hint of impropriety. Even as he watched a couple at another table slide their basket of bread out of the way so they could hold hands, he cautioned himself not to let the setting, the music, the white tablecloths, fool him.

"There *is* one last-minute change you're not going to like," she said. "The central shaft needs to be modified a little. But I think we can still work with the same general plan. It won't affect the floors at all."

He scrolled through the familiar files until he spotted the difference. The emergency stairwell had been moved from the side of the central shaft to the very middle. The shaft itself seemed smaller, or maybe it was because all the other gear they'd filled it with was gone. Now there was empty space, the discs turned to donuts. He looked up from the tablet and saw their waiter approaching.

"What, no lift?" He wanted to make sure he was seeing this right. To the waiter, he asked for a water and said he'd need more time with the menu.

The waiter bowed and left. Anna placed her napkin on the table and slid over to the adjacent chair. "The board said they had their reasons."

"The medical board?" Donald exhaled. He had grown sick of their meddling and their suggestions, but he had given up on fighting with them. He never won. "Shouldn't they be more worried about people falling over these railings and breaking their necks?"

Anna laughed. "You know they're not into that kind of medicine. All they can think about is what these workers might go though, emotionally, if they're ever trapped in there for a few weeks. They wanted the plan to be simpler. More... *open*."

"Open." Donald chuckled and reached for his glass of wine. "And what do they mean, trapped a few weeks? I feel like we're designing something here you could hole up in for a few years."

Anna shrugged. "You're the elected official. I figure you should know more about this government silliness than I do. I'm a consultant. I'm just getting paid to lay out the pipes."

She finished her wine, and the waiter returned with Donald's water and to take their orders. Anna raised her eyebrow, a familiar twitch that begged a question: *Are you ready*? It used to mean much more, Donald thought, as he glanced at the menu.

"How about you pick for me?" he finally said, giving up. The descriptions of the entrées were little help. He supposed a trained chef might understand what the sauces were and what the preparations meant.

Anna ordered, and the waiter feigned appreciation for her selections.

"So now they want a single stairwell, huh?" Donald imagined the concrete needed for this, then thought of a spiral design made of metal. Stronger and cheaper. "We can keep the service lift, right? Why couldn't we slide this over and put it in right here?"

He showed her the tablet. More wine was poured.

"No. No lifts. Keep everything simple and open. That's what they said."

He didn't like this. Even if the thing would never be used, it should be built as if it might. Why else bother? He'd seen a partial list of supplies they were going to stockpile inside. Doing that by stair seemed insane, unless they planned to stock the floors before the prebuilt sections were craned inside. That was more Mick's department. It was one of many reasons he wished his friend were there.

"You know, this is why I didn't go into architecture." He scrolled through their design and saw all the places where it *wasn't their design*. "I remember the first class we had where we had to go out and meet with mock clients, and they always wanted either the impossible or the downright dumb—or both. And that's when I knew it wasn't for me."

"So you went into politics." Anna laughed.

"Yeah. Good point." Donald smiled, saw the irony. "But hey, it worked for your father."

"My dad went into politics because he didn't know what *else* to do. He got out of the army, sank too much money into busted venture after busted venture, then figured he'd serve his country some other way."

She studied him a long moment.

"This *is* his legacy, you know." She leaned forward and rested her elbows on the table, bent a graceful finger at the tablet. "This is one of those things they said would never get done, and he's *doing* it."

Donald put the tablet down and leaned back in his chair. He turned to the side so he could cross his legs. "He keeps telling me the same thing," he said. "That this is our legacy, this project. I told him I feel too young to be working on my crowning achievement already."

Anna smiled. They both took sips of wine. A basket of bread was dropped off, but neither of them reached for it.

"Speaking of legacies and leaving things behind," Anna asked, "is there a reason you and Helen decided to not have kids?"

Donald placed his glass back on the table. Anna lifted the bottle, but he waved her off. "Well, it's not that we don't want them. We just both went directly from grad school to our careers, you know? We kept thinking—"

"That you'll have forever, right? That you'll always have time. There's no hurry."

"No. It's not that—" He rubbed the tablecloth with the pads of his fingers and felt the slick and expensive fabric slide over the other tablecloth hidden below. When they were finished with their meals and out the door, he figured this top layer would be folded back and carried off with their crumbs, a new layer revealed beneath. Like skin. Or the generations. He took a sip of wine, the tannins numbing his lips.

"I think that's it exactly," Anna insisted. "Every generation is waiting longer and longer to pull the trigger. My mom was almost forty when she had me, and that's getting more and more common."

She tucked a loose strand of hair behind her ear.

"Maybe we all think we might be the first generation that simply doesn't die, that lives forever." She raised her eyebrows. "Now we all *expect* to hit a hundred and thirty, maybe longer, like it's our right. And so this is my theory—"

She leaned closer. Donald was already uncomfortable with where the conversation was going. "Children *used* to be our legacy, right? They were our chance to cheat death, to pass these little bits of ourselves along. But now we hope it can simply be *us*."

"You mean like cloning? That's why it's illegal."

"I don't mean cloning—and besides, just because it's illegal, you and I both know people do it." She took a sip of her wine and nodded at a family in a distant booth. "Look. He has daddy's *everything*."

Donald followed her gaze and watched the kid for a moment, then realized she was just making a point.

"Or how about *my* father?" she asked. "Those nano baths, all the stem-cell vitamins he takes. He truly thinks he's gonna live forever. You know he bought a load of stock in one of those cryo firms years back?"

Donald laughed. "I heard. And I heard it didn't work out so well. Besides, they've been trying stuff like that for years—"

"And they keep getting closer," she said. "All they ever needed was a way to stitch up the cells damaged from the freezing, and now that's not so crazy a dream, right?"

"Well, I hope the people who dream such things get whatever it is they're looking for, but you're wrong about us. Helen and I talk about having kids all the time. I know people having their first kid in their fifties. We've got time."

"Mmm." She finished what was in her glass and reached for the bottle. "You think that," she said. "Everyone thinks they've got all the time in the world." She leveled her cool gray eyes at him. "But they never stop to ask just how much time that is."

••••

After dinner, the two of them waited under the awning for Anna's car service. Donald declined to share a ride, saying he needed to get back to the office and would just take a cab. The rain hitting the awning had changed, grown fiercer. Now it sounded like bubble wrap being popped.

Anna's ride squealed to a stop, a shiny black Lincoln, just as Donald's phone began vibrating. He fumbled in his jacket pocket while she leaned in for a hug and kissed his cheek. He felt a flush of heat despite the cool air, saw that it was Mick calling him, and hit the accept button.

"Hey, you just land, or what?"

A pause.

"Land?" Mick sounded confused. There was noise in the background. The driver hurried around the Lincoln to get the door for Anna. "I took a redeye," Mick said. "My flight got in early this morning. I'm just walking out of a movie and saw your texts. What's up?"

Anna turned and waved. Donald waved back.

"You're getting out of a movie? We just wrapped up our meeting at Angelo's. You missed it. Anna said she emailed you like three times—"

He glanced up at the car as Anna drew her leg inside. Just a glimpse of her red heels, and then the driver thumped the door shut. The rain on the tinted glass stood out like jewels embedded in wet obsidian.

"Huh. I must've missed them. Probably went to junk mail. Hey, have you heard of The Wizard of Oz? We just got out of this film, supposedly a remake. If you and I were still in our getting-high days, I would totally force you to blast one with me right now and go to the midnight showing. My mind is totally bent—"

Donald watched as the driver hurried around the car to get out of the rain. That sheet of gleaming black trembled, the jewels scattering as her window lowered a crack. One last wave, a disembodied hand braving the wet and cold, fingers fluttering.

"Yeah, well, those days are long gone, my friend." Donald waved back as the car pulled out into the light traffic. Thunder grumbled in the distance. An umbrella opened with a pop as a gentleman prepared to brave the storm. "Besides," Donald told Mick, "some things are better off back in the past. Where they belong."

# 18
2110 • Silo 1

The exercise room on level twelve smelled of sweat, of having been recently used. A line of iron weights sat in a jumble in one corner, and someone had forgotten their towel. They had left it draped over the bar of the bench press, over a hundred pounds of iron discs still in place.

Troy eyed the mess as he worked the last bolt free from the side of the exercise bike. When the cover plate came off, washers and nuts rained down from recessed holes and bounced across the tile. Troy scrambled for them and pushed the hardware into a tidy pile. He peered inside the bike's innards and saw a large cog, its jagged teeth conspicuously empty.

The chain that did all the work hung slack around the cog's axle. Troy was surprised to see it there, would think the thing ran on belts or...well, he didn't know *how* he expected the bike to work. But this seemed too fragile. Not a good choice for the length of time it would be expected to serve. It was strange, in fact, to think that this machine was already fifty years old—or that it needed to last centuries more.

He wiped his forehead. Sweat was still beading up from the handful of miles he'd gotten in before the machine broke.

Fishing around in the toolbox Jones had loaned him, he found the flathead screwdriver and began levering the chain back onto the cog.

Chains on cogs. *Chains on cogs.* He laughed to himself. Wasn't that the way?

"Excuse me, sir?"

Troy turned to find Jones, his chief mechanic for another week, standing in the gym's doorway.

"Almost done," Troy said. "You need your tools back?"

"Nossir. Dr. Henson is looking for you." He raised his hand, had one of those clunky radios in it.

Troy grabbed an old rag out of the toolbox and wiped the grease from his fingers. This felt good, working on something, getting dirty. It was a welcome distraction, something to do besides checking the blisters in his mouth with a mirror or hanging out in his office or apartment waiting to cry again for no reason.

*This* was what he was supposed to be doing, not leading or being in charge. He was supposed to be the guy coiling the ropes, not the captain.

He left the bike and crossed to his shift mechanic to accept the radio. Troy felt a wave of envy for the older man. He would love to wake up in the morning, put on those blue denim coveralls with the patches on the knees, grab his trusty toolbox, and work down a list of repairs. Anything other than sitting around while he waited on far worse things to break.

Squeezing the button on the side of the radio, he held it up to his mouth.

"This is Troy," he said.

The name sounded weird coming out of his own mouth. He didn't like saying his own name, didn't like hearing it. He wondered what Dr. Henson and the shrinks would say about that.

The radio crackled. "Sir? I hate to disturb you—"

"No, that's fine. What is it?" Troy walked back to the exercise bike and grabbed his towel from the handlebars. He wiped his forehead and saw Jones eyeing the disassembled bike and scattering of tools. The mechanic looked like a starving man gaping at a buffet. When he lifted his brows questioningly, Troy waved his consent.

"We've got a gentleman in our office who's not responding to treatment," Dr. Henson said.

Jones knelt by the bike. He slid his hands inside the machine's cavity like a surgeon reaching into an open abdomen.

A blast of static, and then Dr. Henson continued: "It looks like another deep-freeze. I'll need you to sign the waiver."

Jones glanced up from the bike and frowned at this. Troy rubbed the back of his neck with the towel. He remembered Merriman saying to be careful handing these out. There were plenty of good men who would just as soon sleep through all this mess than serve their shifts.

"You're sure?" he asked.

"We've tried everything. He's been restrained. Security is taking him down the express right now. Can you meet us down here? You'll have to sign off before he can be put away."

"Sure, sure." Troy rubbed his face with his towel, could smell the detergent in the clean cloth cut through the odor of sweat in the room and the tinge of grease from the open bike. Jones grabbed one of the pedals with his thick hands and gave it a turn. The chain was back on the cog, the machine operational again.

"I'll be right down," Troy said before releasing the mic. He handed the radio back to Jones, and the two men exchanged frowns. Some things were a pleasure to fix. Others weren't.

••••

The express had already passed when Troy reached the lifts; he could see the floor display racing down. He pressed the call button for the other one and tried to imagine the sad scene playing out below. Whoever it was had his sympathies.

He shivered violently, blamed it on the cool air in the hallway and his damp skin. A ping-pong ball clocked back and forth in the rec room around the corner, sneakers squeaking as players chased the next shot. From the same room, a television was playing a movie, the sound of a woman's voice. When the ball stopped, the score was called out.

Looking down at his feet, Troy felt self-conscious about his shorts and tee shirt. The only semblance of authority he really felt was lent by his coveralls, but there was no time to ride up and change.

The lift beeped and opened, a conversation inside falling silent. Troy nodded a greeting, and two men in yellow said hello. The three of them rode in silence for a few levels until the men got off on forty-four, a general living level. Before the doors could close, Troy saw a bright ball skitter across the hallway, two men racing after it. There were shouts and laughter followed by guilty silence when they noticed Troy.

The metal doors squeezed shut on the brief glimpse of lower and more normal lives.

With a shudder, the lift sank deeper into the earth. Troy could feel the dirt and concrete squeezing in from all sides, piling up above. Sweat mixed with more sweat and so remained hidden. He was coming out of the other side of the medication, he thought. Every morning, he could feel some semblance of his old self returning, and it lasted longer and longer into the day.

The fifties went by. The lift never stopped on the fifties. Emergency supplies he hoped would never be needed filled the corridors beyond. He remembered parts of the orientation time, back when everyone had been awake. He remembered the code names they came up with for everything, the way new labels obscured the past. There was something here nagging him, but he couldn't place it.

Next were the mechanical spaces and the general storerooms, followed by the two levels that housed the reactor. Finally, the most important storage of all: the Legacy, the deep sleep of men and women in their shiny coffins, the survivors from the *before*, the sailors asleep in their bunks.

There was a jolt of gravity as the lift slowed, a *ding*, doors trembling open. Troy heard a commotion in the doctor's office, Henson barking commands to his assistant. He hurried down the hallway in his gym attire, sweat cooling on his skin.

When he entered the ready room, he saw an elderly man. It was Hal—Troy recognized him from the cafeteria, remembered speaking with him the first day of his shift and several times since. Hal was being restrained on a gurney by two men from

Security. The doctor and his assistant were fumbling through cabinets and drawers, gathering supplies.

"*My name is Carlton!*" Hal roared. He seemed to be coming out of a fog, looked dazed like he had just woken up from a stupor. Troy assumed they would've had him under control to get him down the lift, wondered if he had broken free or come to. Hal's thin arms flailed while unbuckled restraints dangled from the flat table and swayed from the commotion. Henson and his assistant found what they needed and gathered by the gurney. The Security guys grunted with effort. Hal's eyes widened at the sight of the needle the assistant was holding; the fluid inside was a blue the color of open sky.

Dr. Henson looked up and saw Troy standing there in his exercise clothes, paralyzed and watching the scene. Hal screamed once more that his name was Carlton and continued to kick at the air, boots slamming against the table. The two Security men jerked with effort as they held him down.

"A hand?" Henson grunted, teeth clenched as he began to wrestle with one of Hal's arms.

Troy hurried to the gurney and grabbed one of the man's legs. He stood shoulder to shoulder with the Security officers and wrestled a boot while trying not to get kicked. Hal's legs felt like a bird's inside the baggy coveralls, but they kicked like a mule's. His skinny arms stirred the air while one of the officers worked a strap across his thighs. Troy leaned his weight on Hal's shin while a second strap was flapped over.

"What's wrong with him?" he asked. His concerns about himself swiftly subsided in the presence of true madness. Or was this where he was heading?

"Meds aren't taking," Henson said.

*Or he's not taking them*, Troy thought.

The medical assistant used his teeth to pull the cap off the sky-colored syringe. Hal's wrist was pinned. The needle disappeared into his trembling arm, the plunger moving bright blue into his pale and blotchy flesh.

Veins, already purple with effort, deepened in hue.

Troy cringed at the sight of sharp steel being stabbed into Hal's jerking arm—but the power in the old man's legs faded immediately. Everyone seemed to take deep breaths as he wilted into unconsciousness, his head drifting to the side, one last incomprehensible scream fading into a moan, and then a deep and breathy exhalation.

"What the hell?" Troy wiped his forehead with the back of his arm. He was dripping with sweat, partly from the exertion but mostly from the scene of madness, from feeling a man go under like that, sensing the life and will drain from his kicking boots as he was forced asleep. His own body shook with a sudden and violent tremor, gone before he knew it was coming. The doctor glanced up and frowned.

"I apologize for that," Henson said. He glared at the officers, directing his blame.

"We had him no problem," one of them said, shrugging.

Henson turned to Troy. His jowls sagged with disappointment. "I hate to ask you to sign off on this—"

Troy wiped his face with the front of his shirt and nodded. The losses had been accounted for—individual losses as well as silos, spares stocked accordingly—but they all stung.

"Of course," he said. This was his job, right? Sign this. Say these words. Follow the script. It was a joke. They were all reading lines from a play none of them could remember. But he was beginning to. He could *feel* it.

Henson shuffled through a drawer of forms while his assistant unbuckled Hal's coveralls. The men from Security asked if they were needed, checked the restraints a final time, and were waved away. While their boots faded toward the lift, one of them laughed out loud over something the other said, already back to joking.

Troy, meanwhile, lost himself in Hal's slack face, the slight rise and fall of his old and narrow chest. *Here* was the reward for remembering, he thought. This man had woken up from the routine of the asylum. He hadn't gone crazy; he'd had a sudden bout of *clarity*. He'd cracked his eyes and seen through the mist.

Troy tucked his hands in his armpits and tried to remain calm, to remain detached. He didn't want Henson to see his trembling hands or suspect that he'd had glimpses as well.

A clipboard was procured from a peg on the wall, the right form shoved into its metal jaws. Troy was handed a pen. He scratched a name, but it didn't feel right. What was this meaninglessness with a pen when a needle had already bit a man's flesh? This wasn't the deed, these forms and ink. The deed was on a table with a slack jaw and drooping lids.

He handed the clipboard back and watched the two doctors work; he wondered if they felt any of what he felt. What if they were all playing the same part? What if each and every inmate in this asylum was concealing the same doubts, none of them talking because they all felt utterly and completely alone?

"Could you get that one for me?"

The medical assistant was down on his knees, twisting a knob on the base of the table. Troy saw that it was on wheels. The assistant nodded toward Troy's feet.

"Of course." Troy crouched down to free the wheel. He was a part in this. It was his signature on the form. It was him twisting the knob that would free the table and allow it to roll down the hall.

With Hal under, the restraints were loosened, his coveralls peeled off with care. Troy volunteered with the boots, unknotting the laces and setting them aside. There was no need for a paper gown—that was for the modesty of the awake. An IV needle was inserted and taped down; Troy knew it would plug into the pod. He knew what it felt like to have ice crawl through his veins.

When Henson told them everything was ready, Troy helped guide the foot of the table, the assistant doing most of the pushing. They followed the doctor out the door and down the hallway, past the room Troy had woken up in, past his empty and waiting coffin, and further down toward the room that sang out to him most nights, the room he had wanted to visit that first day of his shift, the room that lay full of some forgotten misery that didn't want to be remembered. It was a room for the long-sleeping, and it tugged on his gut similar to how the cafeteria yanked on his soul. It was no wonder he felt torn apart living and working in the numb space in between: there was something at either end of the building calling out to him, some hurt too strong to recall but impossible to ignore.

They brought the gurney to a halt outside the reinforced steel doors of the deep-freeze. Troy studied the doors. They seemed familiar. He seemed to remember speccing something similar for a project once, but that was for a room full of machines. No, computers. Shards of the past came back, slid like ghost ships through the mist.

The keypad on the wall chirped as the doctor entered his code. There was the heavy *thunk* of rods withdrawing into the thick jamb and the hiss and sigh of an unbreathing room as it cracked its mouth.

"The empties are at the end," Henson said, nodding into the distance.

Troy steered while the assistant pushed. Wheels squeaked and squealed, their echoes filling this inner sanctum. Troy felt guilty about the noise, even though the sleep in that room could not be so easily disturbed.

Rows and rows of gleaming and sealed beds marched by. The gurney and the three men seemed to stand still while the pods drifted past. Troy felt numb. He was out of his own body as a memory returned. The room was chilly. His eyes fell to the readout screens on the bases of each pod. There were green lights solid with life, numbers showing the chill of the frozen, no space needed for a pulse or heartbeat, first names only, no last, no way to connect these strangers to their legacy. No way to connect them to what they'd done.

*Cassie, Catherine, Gabriella, Gretchen.*

Made-up names.

*Gwynn. Halley. Heather.*

Everyone in order. No shifts for them. Nothing for the men to fight over. It would all be done in an instant. Step inside the lifeboat, dream a moment, step out onto dry land.

Another Heather. Duplicates without last names. Troy wondered how that would work. He steered blindly between the rows, the doctor and his assistant chatting about the procedure, when a name stabbed at his peripheral, a fierce quake vibrating through his limbs.

*Helen.* And another: *Helen.*

Troy lost his grip on the gurney and nearly fell. The wheels squealed to a stop.

"Sir?"

Two Helens. But before him, on a crisp display showing the frozen temps of a deep, deep slumber, another:

*Helena.*

Troy staggered away from the gurney and the still form of Hal's nakedness. The echo of the old man's feeble screams came back to him, insisting he was someone named Carlton. Troy ran his hands along the curved top of the cryopod. She was *here*. He knew she was, but always in the ephemeral way like how he vaguely knew that his organs were buried within his own body. Except suddenly, everything was exposed. Like skin peeled back, layers of his *being* forgotten. He was invisible, the lies on the surface transparent. He saw his spleen, wet and shiny. Coils of intestine. These things that were a part of him, things tucked away and now resting visible beneath his palm.

"Sir? We really need to keep moving—"

Troy ignored the doctor. He rubbed the glass shield, the cold inside leaching through into his hand, the chill in the air creeping deep into the marrow of his bones. Troy's gut tightened around a memory—

"Sir—"

A spiderweb of frost covered the glass. He wiped the frozen film of condensation away so he could see inside.

"We need to get this man installed—"

Sealed eyes lay inside that cold and dark place. Skin and air held a tint of blue. Blades of ice, like a snow queen's mascara, clung to her lashes. It was a familiar face, but this was not his wife.

"Sir!"

The fist in his gut—that hand that clenched desperately around the nothingness—it stirred. It punched upward into his heart. Troy stumbled, hands slapping at the cold coffin for balance, bile rising in his throat with remembrance, his body searching for some medicine to dissolve.

He heard himself gag, felt his limbs twitch, his knees buckle. He hit the ground between two of the pods and shook violently, spit on his lips, strong memories wrestling with the last residue of weak drugs.

The two men in white barked at each other. Footsteps slapped frosted steel and faded toward the distant and heavy door. Shivers and inhuman gurgles hit his own ears and sounded faintly as though they came from him.

But who was he? What was he doing there? What were any of them doing?

The shakes subsided to a vibration, a bass chord thumbed hard and shivering home from some invisible state. Troy settled into this sonorous tremble, the cold floor distant somehow, his body growing numb as his mind became *aware*.

This was not Helen. His name was not Troy.

He almost had it as feet stomped his way in a hurry. The name was on his tongue as the needle bit his flesh.

*Donny.*

But that wasn't right, either.

And then the darkness took him, the cold enveloping him like a hoary cocoon, tightening down around anything from his past that his mind deemed too awful to bear.

# 19
## 2052 • Fulton County, Georgia

Some mash-up of music festival, family reunion, and state fair had descended on the southernmost corner of Fulton County. For the past two weeks, Donald had watched while colorful tents sprang up over a brand-new nuclear containment facility. Fifty state flags flew over fifty depressions in the earth. Stages had been erected, an endless parade of supplies flowing over the rolling hills, golf carts and four-wheelers forming convoys like ants marching back to their nests, their mandibles full of food, boxes, Tupperware containers, baskets of vegetables—some even pulled small enclosed trailers loaded with livestock.

The foodies were out in droves. Farmers' markets had been staked out in winding corridors of tents and booths, chickens clucking and pigs snorting, children petting rabbits, dogs on leashes. Owners of the latter guided dozens of breeds through the crowds. Tails wagged happily, and wet noses sniffed the air.

On Georgia's main stage, a local rock band performed a sound check. When they fell quiet to adjust levels, Donald could hear the twangs of bluegrass spilling over from the general direction of North Carolina's delegation. In the opposite direction, someone was giving a speech on Florida's stage while lines of ants moved supplies over the rise, and families spread blankets and picnicked on the banks of sweeping bowls. The hills, Donald saw, formed stadium seating, as if they'd been designed for the task.

What he couldn't figure was where they were putting all those supplies. The tents seemed to keep gobbling them up with no end in sight. The four-wheelers with their little boxed trailers had been rumbling up and down the slopes the entire two weeks he'd been there helping prep for the national convention.

A set of brakes squealed beside him as Mick rumbled to a stop, sitting atop one of the ubiquitous ATVs. He grinned at Donald like a guilty frat boy and goosed the throttle while still holding the brakes. The Honda lurched, tires growling against the dirt.

"Wanna go for a ride?" he yelled.

"Where to?" Donald screamed back. The rock band resumed its sound check, the Honda blatting as Mick worked the throttle.

"South Carolina," Mick said, smiling. He scooted forward on the seat to make room.

"You got enough gas to make it there?" Donald held his friend's shoulder and stepped on the second set of pegs, threw his leg over the seat.

"It's just over that hill, you idiot."

Donald resisted the urge to assure Mick he'd been joking. He held on to the metal rack behind him as Mick gave it gas and shifted through to third gear. His friend stuck to the dusty highway between the tents until they reached the grass, then angled toward the South Carolina delegation, the tops of the buildings of downtown Atlanta visible off to one side.

Mick turned his head as the Honda climbed the hill. "When is Helen getting here?" he yelled.

Donald leaned forward. He loved the feel of the cool October morning air as the ATV created a breeze. It reminded him of Savannah that time of year, the chill of a sunrise on the beach. He had just been thinking of Helen when Mick asked about her.

"Tomorrow," he shouted. "She's coming on a bus with the delegates from Savannah."

They crested the hill, and Mick throttled back and steered along the ridgeline. They passed a loaded-down four-wheeler heading in the opposite direction. The network of ridges formed an interlocked maze of highways high above each containment facility's sunken bowl.

Peering into the distance—the bumps in the trail traveling up through the metal cargo rack and into his arms—Donald watched the ballet of scooting ATVs weave across the landscape. One day, he imagined, the flat roads on top of the hills would rumble with much larger trucks bearing hazardous waste and radiation warnings. This would be the last time civilians could march up and down grass hillsides designed not for stadium seating but simply because all the soil dug up from below had to go *somewhere*.

And yet, seeing the flags waving over the Florida delegation to one side and the Georgia stage to the other, and noting the way the slopes would carry record crowds and afford everyone a perfect view of each stage, Donald couldn't help but think that all the happy accidents had some larger purpose. It was as if the facility had been planned from the beginning to serve the 2052 Democratic National Convention, as if it had been built with more than its original goal in mind.

••••

A large blue flag with a white tree and crescent moon swayed lazily over the South Carolina stage. Mick parked the four-wheeler in a sea of ATVs ringing the large hospitality tent. Donald watched his friend pocket the key, even though all of the vehicles were on loan. He supposed it prevented someone from taking their ride by mistake.

Following Mick through the parked vehicles, Donald saw that they were heading toward a smaller tent, which was swallowing a ton of traffic.

"What kind of errand are we on?" he asked.

Not that it mattered—in recent days they'd done a little of everything around the facility: running bags of ice to various state headquarters, meeting with congressmen and senators to see if they needed anything, making sure all the volunteers and delegates were settling into their trailers okay, whatever the Senator needed.

"Oh, we're just taking a little tour," Mick said cryptically. He waved Donald into the small tent where workers were filing through in one direction with their arms loaded and coming out the other side empty-handed.

In comparison, he and Mick looked conspicuously lazy—or perhaps important—as they passed through with nothing.

The inside of the small tent was lit up with flood lights,

the ground packed hard from the traffic, the grass matted flat. A concrete ramp led deep into the earth, workers with volunteer badges trudging up one side. Mick jumped into the line heading down.

Donald knew where they were going. He recognized the ramp. He hurried up beside Mick.

"This is one of the rod storage facilities." He couldn't hide the excitement in his voice, didn't even try. He'd been dying to see the *other* design, either on paper or in person. "Can we just go *in*?"

As if to answer, Mick started down the ramp, blending with the others.

"I begged for a tour the other day," Donald hissed, "but Thurman spouted all this national security crap—"

Mick laughed. Halfway down the slope, the roof of the tent seemed to recede into the darkness above, the concrete walls on either side funneling the workers toward the gaping steel doors.

"You're not gonna get inside one of those other facilities," Mick told him. He put his hand on Donald's back and ushered him through the industrial-looking and familiar entrance chamber. The foot traffic ground to a halt as people took turns entering or leaving through the small hatch ahead. Donald felt turned around.

"Wait." Donald caught glimpses through the hatch. "This is my design."

They shuffled forward. Mick made room for the people coming out. He had a hand on Donald's shoulder, guiding him along.

"What're we doing here?" Donald asked. He could've sworn his bunker design was in the bowl set aside for Tennessee. Then again, they'd been making so many last-minute changes the past weeks—and the CAD-FAC design made it easy to get turned around—maybe he'd been mixed up.

"Anna told me you wimped out and skipped the tour of this place."

"That's bullshit." Donald stopped at the oval hatch. He recognized every rivet—more from his drawings than from passing through a few weeks before. He waved the inside people out, allowing them to pass through the tight squeeze first. "Why would she say that? I was right here. I cut the damn ribbon."

Mick pushed at his back. "Go. You're holding up the line."

"I don't want to go." He waved more people out. The workers behind Mick shifted in place, heavy Tupperware containers in their hands. "I saw the top floor," he said. "That was enough."

His friend clasped his neck with one hand and gripped his wrist with the other. As his head was bent forward—like a perp shoved into a squad car—Donald had to move along to avoid falling on his face. He tried to reach for the jamb of the interior door, but Mick had his wrist.

"I want you to see what you *built*," his friend said.

Donald stumbled through to the security office. He and Mick stepped aside to let the congestion they'd caused ease past.

"I've been looking at this damn thing every day for three years," Donald said. He patted his pocket for his pills, wondered if it was too soon to take another. What he didn't tell Mick was that he'd forced himself to envision his design being *above* ground the entire time he'd worked on it, more a skyscraper than a buried straw. No way could he share that with his best friend, tell him how terrified he felt right then with no more than ten meters of dirt and concrete over his head. He seriously doubted Anna had used the phrase "wimped out," but that's exactly what he had done after working those oversized shears. While the Senator led dignitaries through the complex, Donald had gone up to find a patch of grass with nothing but bright blue above while the sweat cooled from his neck and he gasped for fresh air.

"This is really fucking important," Mick said. He snapped his fingers in front of Donald. Two lines of workers filed past. Beyond them, a man sat in a small cubicle, a brush in one hand and a can of paint in the other. He was painting a set of steel bars a flat gray. A technician behind him was wiring something on the wall. Not everything looked like it was being finished precisely the way Donald had drawn it.

"Donny, listen to me. I'm dead serious. Today is the last day we can have this talk, okay? I need you to see what you built."

Donald tore his gaze away from the workers. He shouldn't be surprised that there were last minute details that needed attending to. The entire project had been rushed right up to the end, every deadline missed as they fought to catch up. He had suggested they wait and complete the build *after* the national convention. The Senator and a few others had nearly blown their tops.

Looking to Mick, he saw a similar mask of seriousness. His friend's permanent and mischievous grin was gone, his eyebrows tilted. He looked, if anything, sad.

"Will you please come inside?" he asked.

Donald wanted to laugh and point out that he already *was* inside. But he knew what Mick meant. He meant deeper. Taking a full breath and fighting the urge to rush out to the hills and fresh air, away from the stifling crowds, Donald found himself agreeing. It was the look on Mick's face, the feeling that he needed to tell Donald about a loved one who had just passed away, something deathly serious.

Mick patted his shoulder in gratitude as Donald nodded. He turned and merged with the line heading through the security office's inner door, and Donald felt like he was seeing one of the thousands of rendered walk-throughs he'd performed in AutoCAD. It helped to imagine this. He wasn't below the earth and concrete at all—he was in his office on Capitol Hill. He was at his desk, working his mouse, sending his bodiless avatar through his blueprints one final time. So when he gasped for air, he imagined the window behind his desk was open, the sounds of D.C. traffic wafting through on the fresh breeze—

"This way."

Mick led him toward the central shaft. Donald slid his imaginary mouse forward and followed. They passed through the cafeteria, which was being used. It made sense. Workers sat at tables and ate off plastic trays, taking a break. The smell of food drifted from the kitchens beyond. Donald laughed. He never thought they'd be used at all. At least they would have this one go. Again, it felt like the convention had given this place a purpose. It made him happy. He thought of the entire complex devoid of life one day, all the workers milling about outside storing away nuclear rods, Atlanta buzzing with its everyday routine, while this massive building, a skyscraper that would have touched the clouds had it been placed above ground, would sit perfectly empty, plunged into the dirt like a forgotten needle.

Down a short hallway, the tile gave way to metal grating, and a broad cylinder dove straight through the heart of the facility. Anna had been right. It really was worth seeing. He really had wimped out.

They reached the railing of the central shaft, and Donald paused to peer over. The vast height made him forget for a moment that he was underground. On the other side of the landing, a conveyor lift rattled on its gears while a never ending series of flat loading trays spun empty over the top. It reminded Donald of the buckets on a waterwheel. The trays flopped over before descending back down through the building.

The men and women from outside deposited each of their containers onto one of the empty trays before turning and heading back out. Donald looked for Mick and saw him disappearing down the staircase.

He hurried after, his fear of being buried alive chasing him. "Hey!"

His shoes slapped the freshly painted stairs, the diamond plating keeping him from skidding off in his haste. He caught up with Mick as they made a full circuit of the thick inner post. Tupperware containers full of emergency supplies—supplies

Donald figured would rot, unused—drifted eerily downward beyond the rail as Donald raced to match Mick's pace.

"I don't want to go any deeper than this," he insisted.

"Two levels down," Mick called back up. "C'mon, man, I want you to see."

Donald numbly obeyed. It would've been worse to make his way out alone.

At the first landing they came to, a worker stood by the conveyor with some sort of gun. As the next container passed by, he shot its side with a flash of red, the scanner buzzing. The worker leaned on the railing, waiting for the next one while the container continued its ratcheting plummet.

"Did I miss something?" Donald asked. "Are we still fighting deadlines? What's with all the supplies?"

Mick shook his head. "Deadlines, lifelines," he said.

At least, that's what Donald thought his friend said. Mick seemed lost in thought.

They spiraled down another level, ten more meters of reinforced concrete between, thirty-three feet of wasted depth, all according to idiotic specifications that he knew all too well.

The next landing looked the same as the last. A young woman stood there with her scanner, two Tupperware containers stacked up by her feet. Her gun buzzed as she targeted the next one rumbling down the line. A good-looking young man came out of a pair of hinged doors and grabbed the top container. The two shared a few words while Mick grabbed the open door and waved Donald through.

Donald knew the floor. And not just from the plans he'd drawn. They had toured a floor like this in the factory where it had been built.

"I've been here before," he told Mick.

Mick nodded. He waved Donald down the hallway until it made a turn. Mick picked one of the doors, seemingly at random, and opened it for Donald. Most of the floors had been pre-fabbed before being craned into place. If that wasn't that exact floor the two of them had toured, it had been one of the many just like it.

Once Donald was inside, Mick flicked on the apartment's overhead lights and closed the door. Donald was surprised to see that the bed was made. Stacks of linen were piled up in a chair. They could be in a tiny hotel room in New York City or Tokyo, and he wouldn't know the difference. Mick grabbed the linens and moved them to the floor. He sat down and nodded toward the foot of the bed.

Donald ignored him and poked his head into the small bathroom. "This is actually pretty cool to see," he told his friend. He reached out and turned the knob on the sink, expecting nothing. When clear water gurgled out, he found himself laughing.

"I knew you'd dig it once you saw it," Mick said quietly.

Donald caught sight of himself in the mirror, the joy still on his face. He tended to forget how the corners of his eyes wrinkled up when he smiled. He touched his hair, sprinkles of gray even though he had another five years before he was over that proverbial hill. His job was aging him prematurely. He had feared it might.

"Pretty cool that we built this, huh?"

Mick was still waiting for him to sit. Donald turned and joined his friend in the tight quarters. He wondered if it was the work they'd been elected to perform that had aged them both or if it had been this one project, this all-consuming build.

"I appreciate you forcing me down here." He almost added that he would love to see the rest, but he figured that would be pushing it. Besides, the crew back in the Georgia tents were probably looking for them already.

"Look," Mick said, "there's something I want to tell you."

Donald peered down at his friend, who seemed to be searching for the words. He glanced at the door. Mick was silent. Donald finally relented and sat at the foot of the bed.

"What's up?" he asked.

But he thought he knew. The Senator had included Mick in his other project, the one that had filled Donald's head with nuttiness and had driven him to the doctor. Donald thought of the thick book he had largely memorized, the last years spent reading little else. Mick had been doing the same. And he'd brought him there not just to let him see what they'd accomplished, but to find a spot of perfect privacy, a place where secrets could be divulged. He patted his pocket where he kept his pills, the ones that kept his thoughts from running off to dangerous places. He considered offering one to Mick.

"Hey," Donald said, "I don't want you saying anything you're not supposed to—"

Mick looked up, eyes wide with surprise.

"You don't need to say *anything*, Mick. Assume I know what *you* know."

Mick shook his head sadly. "You don't," he said.

"Well, assume it anyway." He waved his hands like an umpire calling a runner safe at the plate. "I don't want to know anything."

"I *need* you to know—"

"I'd rather not—"

"It's not a secret, man. It's just...I want you to know that I love you like a brother. I always have."

The two of them sat in silence. Donald glanced toward the door. It was uncomfortable, that moment, but it somehow filled his heart to hear Mick say it.

"Look—" Donald started.

"I know I'm always hard on you," Mick said. "And hell, I'm sorry. I really do look up to you. And Helen—" Mick turned to the side and scratched at his cheek. "I'm so damn happy for the two of you."

Donald reached across the narrow space and squeezed his friend's arm.

"You're a good friend, Mick. I'm glad we've had this time together, the last few years, running for office like idiots, building this—"

Mick nodded. "Yeah. Me too. But listen, I didn't bring you down here to get all sappy like this." He reached for his cheek again, and Donald saw that he was wiping at his eyes. "I had a talk with Thurman last night. He—a few months ago, he offered me a spot on a team, a top team, and I told him last night that I'd rather you take it."

"What? A committee?" Donald couldn't imagine his friend giving up an appointment, *any* kind of appointment. "Which one?"

Mick shook his head. "No, something else."

"What?" Donald asked.

"Look," Mick said, "when you find out about it, and you

understand what's going on, I want you to think of me right here." Mick glanced around the room. There were a few breaths of complete silence punctuated by drips of water from the bathroom sink.

"If I could choose anywhere to be, *anywhere* in the coming years, it would be right down here with the first group."

"Okay. Yeah, I'm not sure what you mean—"

"You will. Just remember this, all right? That I love you like a brother and that everything happens for a reason. I wouldn't have wanted it any other way. For you or for Helen."

"Okay—" Donald smiled. He couldn't tell if Mick was fucking with him or if his friend had consumed a few too many Bloody Marys from the hospitality tent that morning.

"All right." Mick stood abruptly. He certainly moved as though he were sober. "Let's get the fuck out of here. This place gives me the creeps."

Donald laughed. Mick threw open the door and flicked off the lights.

"Wimping out, eh?" Donald called after his friend.

Mick punched him in the arm as the two of them headed back down the hallway. The young man from earlier passed by with a tub in his hands. Behind them, they left the small, random apartment in darkness, its little sink dripping. And Donald tried to sort out how he'd gotten turned around, how the Tennessee tent where he'd cut the ribbon had become the one from South Carolina. He almost had it, his subconscious flashing to a delivery of goods, to fifty times more fiber optic than he needed, but the connection was lost.

Meanwhile, containers loaded with supplies rumbled down the mammoth shaft. And empty trays rattled up.

# 20
2110 • Silo 1

Troy woke up in a fog. He lifted his hands and groped in front of his face, expecting to find the chill of icy glass, the press of domed steel, the doom of a deep-freeze. Instead, his hands waved in empty air. The clock beside his bed came into focus. It was a little after three. The PM light was unlit. He had the grogginess and headache of a hangover, the midnight confusion of sleeping with the flu, the hours meaningless in the wake of some sudden fever.

He sat up, the springs of his bed squeaking. He had on a pair of gym shorts, couldn't remember changing the night before, couldn't remember going to bed. There was something else he needed to remember and couldn't. Planting his feet on the floor, he rested his elbows on his knees, sunk his head into his palms, and sat there a moment. His entire body ached. There was something he was supposed to be doing.

After a few minutes slipped by, he dressed himself in the dark, buckling up his coveralls. Light would be bad for his headache. It wasn't a theory he needed to test.

The hallway outside was still dimmed for the evening, just bright enough to grope one's way to the shared bathrooms and not a watt more. Troy stole down the hall, not needing to pee, and headed for the lift.

He hit the "Up" button, hesitated, wasn't sure if that was right. He pressed the "Down" button as well.

It was too early to go into his office, not unless he wanted to fiddle on the computer. He wasn't hungry, but he could go up and watch the sun rise. The late shift would be up there drinking coffee. Or he could hit the rec room and go for a jog. That would mean going back to his room to change.

The lift arrived with a beep while he was still deciding. Both lights went off, the up and the down. He could take this lift anywhere.

Troy stepped inside. He didn't know where he wanted to go.

The elevator doors closed. It waited on him patiently. Eventually, he figured, it would whisk off to heed some other call, pick up a person with purpose, someone with a destination. He could stand there and do nothing and let that other soul decide. He could just go along for the ride.

Running his finger across the buttons, he tried to remember what was on each level. There was a lot he'd memorized, but not everything he knew felt accessible. He had a sudden urge to head for one of the lounges and watch TV, just let the hours slide past until he finally needed to be somewhere. This was how the shift was supposed to go. Waiting and then doing. Sleeping and then waiting. Make it to dinner and then make it to bed. The end was always in sight. There was nothing to rebel against, just a routine, until the now faded into the past, and the future wilted and died.

The elevator shivered into motion before he could decide. Troy jerked his hand away from the buttons and took a step back. The elevator didn't show where they were going. It felt like they had started down.

Only a few floors passed before the lift lurched to a halt. The doors opened on a lower apartment level. A familiar face from the cafeteria, a man in reactor red, smiled as he stepped inside.

"Morning," he said.

Troy nodded.

The man turned and jabbed one of the lower buttons, one of the reactor levels. He studied the otherwise blank array, turned and gave Troy a quizzical look.

"You feeling okay, sir?"

"Hmm? Oh, yeah."

Troy leaned forward and pressed sixty-eight. The man's concern for his well-being must've had him thinking of the doctor, even though Henson wouldn't be on shift for several hours.

"Must not have taken the first time," he explained, glancing at the button.

"Mmm."

The silence lasted one or two floors.

"How much longer you got?" the reactor mechanic asked.

"Me? Just another couple o' weeks. How about you?"

"I just got on a week ago. But this is my second shift."

"Oh?"

The lights counted downward in floors but upward in number. Troy didn't like this; he felt like the lowest level should be level 1. They should count *up*. He wasn't sure why this annoyed him.

"Is the second shift easier?" he asked. The question came out unbidden. It was as though the part of him dying to know was more awake than the part of him praying for silence.

The mechanic seemed to consider this.

"I wouldn't say it's easier. How about…less uncomfortable?" He laughed quietly. Troy felt their arrival in his knees, gravity tugging on him. The door beeped open.

"Have a good one," the mechanic said. They hadn't shared their names. "In case I don't see you again."

Troy raised his palm. "Next time," he said. The man stepped out, and the doors winked shut on the halls to the power plant. With a hum, the elevator continued its descent.

Troy's stomach was in a knot. It wasn't hunger. It was something else. Something stronger than worry.

The doors dinged on the medical level. Troy stepped out. He felt the hallways calling someone else's name. That was his imagination, but there were also real voices down the corridor, two men chatting. He stepped quietly across the tile. He remembered picking out tile like this once. Somehow, he knew the name of the pale green paint on the upper half of the walls. Sea foam. The lower half was something else—he couldn't recall.

A female voice. It wasn't a conversation; it was an old movie. Troy peeked into the main office and saw a man lounging on a gurney, his back turned, a TV set up in the corner. Troy tiptoed past so as not to disturb him. He supposed that there were positions here—like the reactor mechanics—that were much more important than his own, jobs that required constant care. No one stayed up all night in *his* office, that was for sure.

The hallway split before him. He imagined the layout, could picture the pie-shaped storerooms, the rows of deep-freeze coffins, the tubes and pipes that led from the walls to the bases, from the bases into the people inside.

He stopped at one of the heavy doors and tried his code. The light winked from red to green. He dropped his hand, didn't need to enter this room, didn't feel the urge, just wanted to see if it would work.

He meandered down the hall past a few more doors. Wasn't he just here? Had he ever left? Hours of darkness lay between him and some event. His arm throbbed. He rolled back his sleeve and saw a spot of blood, a circle of redness around a pinprick scab.

If something bad had happened, he couldn't remember. That part of him had been choked off.

Adjusting his sleeve, he tried his code on this other pad, this other door, and waited for the light to turn green. Something was calling him. This time, he pushed the button that opened the door. He didn't know what it was, but there was something inside that he needed to see.

# 21
2052 • The Hills Above Silo 1

Light rains on the morning of the Convention left the man-made hills soggy, the new grass slick, but did little to erode the general festivities. Parking lots had been emptied of construction vehicles and mud-caked pickups. Now they held hundreds of idling buses and a handful of sleek black limos, the latter splattered ignobly with mud.

The lot where temporary trailers had served as offices and living quarters for construction crews had been handed over to the staffers, volunteers, delegates, and dignitaries who had labored for weeks to bring the day to fruition. The area was dotted with welcoming tents that served as the headquarters for the event coordinators. Throngs of new arrivals filed from the buses and made their way through the CAD-FAC's security station. Massive fences bristled with coils of razor wire and seemed outsized and ridiculous for the convention but made sense for the storing of nuclear material. These barriers and gates held at bay an odd union of protestors: those on the Right who disagreed with the facility's current purpose and those on the Left who feared its future one.

There had never been a National Convention with such energy, such crowds. Downtown Atlanta loomed far beyond the treetops, but the city that had ages ago hosted a Summer Olympics seemed far removed from the sudden bustle in lower Fulton County. The location allowed use of its airport but did very little for hotel owners and restaurateurs, not like those business owners had come to expect and appreciate from the four-year gathering of each political party.

Donald shivered beneath his umbrella at the top of a knoll and thought of the hundred thousand screaming fans who used to descend on Athens for home football games. He hated those weekends. The noise and traffic, the drunks and their music. As an undergrad at Georgia, he had kept a schedule of the home games on his fridge so he'd know when to prepare. He would hit the grocery store like it was the end of the world and lock himself in his dorm room for the duration, not coming out until the noise had subsided and the planet felt safe again.

For some reason, he didn't mind these crowds. They were people like him. He gazed out over the sea of people gathering across the hills, heading toward whichever stage flew their state's flag, umbrellas bobbing and jostling like water bugs.

Somewhere, a marching band blared a practice tune and stomped another hill into mud. There was a sense in the air that the world was about to change—a woman was about to win the Democratic nomination for president, only the second such nomination in Donald's lifetime. And if the pollsters could be believed, this one had more than a chance. Unless the war in Iran took a sudden turn, a milestone would be reached, a final glass ceiling shattered. And it would happen right there in those grand divots in the earth, this landmark project that would see an end to energy dependence and a brave new future for the beleaguered art of splitting atoms.

As more buses churned through the lot and disgorged their passengers, Donald pulled out his phone and checked the time. He still had an error icon, the network choked to death from the demand. He was surprised, with so much other careful planning, that the committee hadn't accounted for this and erected a temporary tower or two.

"Congressman Keene?"

Donald startled and turned to find Anna walking along the ridgeline toward him. He glanced down toward the Georgia stage but didn't see her ride. He was surprised she would just walk up. And yet, it was like her to do things the difficult way.

"I couldn't tell if that was you," she said, smiling. "Everyone has the same umbrella."

"Yeah, it's me." He took a deep breath, found his chest still felt constricted with nerves whenever he saw her, like any conversation could get him into trouble.

Anna stepped close as if she expected him to share his umbrella. He moved it to his other hand to give her more space, the drizzle peppering his exposed arm. He scanned the bus lot and searched impossibly for any sign of Helen. She should have been there by now.

"This is gonna be a mess," Anna said.

"It's supposed to clear up."

Someone on the North Carolina stage checked their microphone with a squawk of feedback.

"We'll see."

Anna wrapped her coat tighter against the early morning breeze. "Isn't Helen coming?"

"Yeah. Senator Thurman insisted. She's not gonna be happy when she sees how many people are here. She hates crowds. She won't be happy about the mud, either."

Anna laughed. "I wouldn't worry about the conditions of the grounds after this."

Donald thought about all the loads of radioactive waste that would be trucked in. "Yeah." He thought he saw her point.

Turning away from the parking lot for a moment, he peered down the hill toward the Georgia stage. It would also be the site of the first national gathering of delegates later that day, all the most important people under one tent. Behind the stage and among the smoking food tents, the only sign of the underground containment facility was a small concrete tower rising up from the ground, a bristle of antennas sprouting from the top. Donald thought of how much work it would take to haul away all the flags and soaked buntings before the first of those spent fuel rods could finally be brought in.

"It's weird to think of a few thousand people from the state of Tennessee stomping around on top of something *we* designed," Anna said. Her arm brushed against Donald's. He stood perfectly still, wondering if it had been an accident. "I wish you'd seen more of the place."

Donald shivered, more from fighting to remain still than from the cold and moist morning air. He hadn't told anyone about Mick's tour the day before. It felt too sacred. He would probably tell Helen about it and no one else. "It's crazy how much time went into something nobody will ever use," he said.

Anna murmured her agreement. Her arm was still touching his. There was no sign of Helen making her way through the security complex. Donald felt irrationally that he would somehow spot her among the crowds. He usually could. He remembered the high balcony of a place they'd stayed in during their honeymoon in Hawaii. Even from up there, he could spot her taking her early morning walks along the foam line, looking for seashells. There might be a few hundred strollers out on the beach, and his eyes would be immediately drawn to her form, her singular gait.

"It's weird how much pressure was on us to get everything right, don't you think?"

"Mmm," Anna said.

"I guess the only way they were going to build any of this was if we gave them the right kind of insurance." Donald repeated what the Senator had told him, but it still didn't feel right.

"People want to feel safe," Anna said. "They want to know, if the worst thing possible happens, they'll have someone—*something* to fall back on."

There was pressure against his arm. Definitely not an accident, not a breeze or gust of wind pushing her into him. Donald felt himself withdraw and knew she would sense it, too.

"I was really hoping to tour one of the *other* bunkers," he said, changing the subject. "It'd be cool to see what the other teams came up with. Apparently, though, I don't have the clearance."

Anna laughed. "I tried the same thing. I'm dying to see our competition. But I can understand them being sensitive. There's a lot of eyes on this joint." She leaned into him, ignoring the space he'd made.

"Don't you feel that?" she asked, glancing up at the bottom of the umbrella. "Like there's some huge bull's eye over this place? I mean, even with the fences and walls down there, you can bet the whole world is gonna be keeping an eye on what happens here."

Donald nodded. He knew she wasn't talking about the convention but about what the place would be used for afterward.

"Hey, it looks like I've got to get back down there."

He turned to follow her gaze, saw Senator Thurman climbing the hill on foot, a massive black golf umbrella shedding the rain around him. The man seemed impervious to the mud and grime in a way no one else was, the same way he seemed oblivious to the passing decades.

Anna reached over and squeezed Donald's arm. "Congrats again. It was fun working together on this."

"Same," he said. "We make a good team."

She smiled. He wondered for a moment if she would lean over and kiss his cheek. It would feel natural in that moment, and then that moment irised shut. Anna left his protective cover and headed off toward the Senator.

Thurman lifted his umbrella and smiled at his daughter, and Donald watched as he tried to make her take the umbrella from him, but she refused in a way that he knew quite well. Stubborn and proud. Thurman kissed his daughter's cheek and watched her descend the hill a ways, then hiked up to join Donald.

They stood beside each other a pause, their umbrellas overlapping, the rain dripping off the Senator's and onto Donald's with a muted patter.

"Sir," Donald finally said. He felt newly comfortable in the man's presence. The last two weeks had been like summer camp, where being around the same people almost every hour of the day brought a level of familiarity and intimacy that knowing them casually for years could never match. There was something about forced confinement that really brought people together. Beyond the obvious, physical ways.

"Damn rain," was Thurman's reply.

"You can't control for everything," Donald said.

The Senator grunted as if he disagreed. "Helen not here yet?"

"Nossir." Donald fished in his pocket and felt for his phone. "I'll message her again in a bit. Not sure if my texts are getting through or not—the networks are absolutely crushed. I'm pretty sure this many people descending on this corner of the county is unprecedented."

"Well, this will be an unprecedented day," Thurman said. "Nothing like it ever before."

"It was mostly your doing, sir. I mean, not just building this place, but choosing to not run. This country could've been yours for the taking this year."

The Senator laughed. "That's true most years, Donny. But I've learned to set my sights higher than that."

Donald shivered again. He couldn't remember the last time the Senator had called him that. Maybe that first meeting in his office, more than two years ago? The old man seemed unusually tense or oddly relaxed. It was strange that Donald couldn't tell which.

"When Helen gets here, I want you to come down to the state tent and see me, okay?"

Donald pulled out his phone and checked the time. "You know I'm supposed to be at the Tennessee tent in an hour, right?"

"There's been a change of plans. I want you to stay close to home. Mick is going to cover for you over there, which means I need you with me."

"Are you sure? I was supposed to meet with—"

"I know. This is a promotion, trust me. I want you and Helen near the Georgia stage with me. And look—"

The Senator turned to face him. Donald peeled his eyes away from the last of the unloading buses. The rain had picked up a little.

"You've contributed more to this day than you know," Thurman said.

"Sir?"

"The world is going to change today, Donny. You deserve this."

Donald wondered if the Senator had been skipping his nanobath treatments. His eyes seemed dilated and focused on something in the distance. He appeared older, somehow.

"I'm not sure I understand—"

"You will. Oh, and a surprise visitor is coming. She should be here anytime." He smiled. "The national anthem starts at noon. There'll be a flyover from the 141st after that. I want you nearby when that happens."

Donald nodded. He had learned when to stop asking questions and just do what the Senator expected of him.

"Yessir," he said, shivering against the cold.

Senator Thurman left, and the sound of the rain on Donald's umbrella shifted with the new bombardment from above. Turning his back to the stage, Donald scanned the last of the buses and wondered where in the world Helen was.

# 22
2110 • Silo 1

Troy walked down the line of cryopods as if he knew where he was going. It was just like how his hand had drifted to the button that brought him to that floor. There were made-up names on each of the panels. He knew this somehow. He remembered coming up with his name. It had something to do with his wife, some way to honor her, or some kind of secret and forbidden link so that he might one day remember.

This all lay in the past, deep in the mist, a dream forgotten. Before his shift there had been an orientation. There were familiar books to read and re-read. That's when he had chosen his name.

A bitter explosion on his tongue brought him to a halt. It was the taste of a pill dissolving. Troy stuck out his tongue and scraped it with his fingers, but there was nothing there but a memory of forgetting. He could feel the ulcers on his gums against his teeth but couldn't recall how they'd formed.

He walked on. Something wasn't right. These things weren't supposed to come back. He pictured himself on a gurney, screaming, someone strapping him down, stabbing him with needles. That wasn't him. He was holding that man's boots.

Troy stopped at one of the pods and checked the name. Helen. There was something wrong. His gut lurched and groped for its medicine. He didn't want to remember. That was a secret ingredient: the *not wanting to remember*. Those were the parts that slipped away, the parts the drugs wrapped their tentacles around and pulled beneath the surface. But now, there was some small part of him that was dying to know, some shard that wanted to rise up through the dark and murky waters. It was a nagging doubt, a feeling of having left some important piece of himself behind. And if the only way to resurface was to bob up as a corpse, this part of him didn't mind. It was willing to drown the rest of him for the answers.

The frost on the glass wiped away with a squeak. He didn't recognize this person, but he was close to remembering. He tried the next one.

What had the orientation been about? How to do new jobs. Some of them already knew, were prepared. Troy had spent two years studying for a similar job. Different but similar. He should have been the head of a *single* silo, not all of them. This was too much.

He remembered packed halls of people crying, grown men sobbing, pills that dried their eyes. Fearsome clouds rose on a videoscreen, a view of the outside, of what they'd done. The suffering and the medicine were caustic together. They made people forget. Troy remembered thinking the bombs were useful more for their fear than the harm they contained. They were a prop. Flesh for the forgetting, for the medicine to sink its teeth into.

The women were put away for safety. That's how the deep-freeze was explained: like lifeboats, women and children first.

Troy remembered. It wasn't an accident. He remembered a talk in another pod, a bigger pod in the shape of a pill, about the coming end of the world, about making *room*, about ending it all before it ended on its own.

A controlled explosion. Bombs were sometimes used to put out fires.

He remembered clouds pushed aside by other clouds. Decoys. The machines were already in the air. He could taste them on his tongue, remembered urine the color of charcoal.

Troy wiped another frost-covered sheet of glass. The sleeping form in the next chamber had eyelashes that glittered with ice. She was a stranger. He moved on. It was coming back to him. His arm throbbed. The shivers were gone.

Troy remembered a calamity, but it was all for show. The real threat was in the air, invisible. The bombs were to get people to move, to make them afraid, to get them crying and forgetting. People had spilled like marbles down a bowl. Not a bowl, a *funnel*. And the air had erupted on cue, invisibly. Someone explained why they were spared. He remembered a white fog, walking through a white fog. The death was already in them. Troy remembered a taste on his tongue metallic.

The ice on the next pane was already disturbed, had been wiped away by someone recently. Beads of condensation stood like tiny lenses warping the light. He rubbed the glass and knew what had happened. He saw the woman inside with the auburn hair that she sometimes kept in a bun. This was not his wife. This was someone who wanted that, wanted *him* like that. The name meant nothing. The name was a reminder to them both.

"Hello?"

Troy turned toward the voice. The night shift doctor was heading his way, weaving between the pods, coming for him. Troy clasped his hand over the soreness on his arm. He didn't want to be taken again. They couldn't make him forget.

"Sir, you shouldn't be in here."

Troy didn't answer. The doctor stopped at the foot of the pod. Inside, a woman who wasn't his wife lay in slumber. Wasn't his wife, but had wanted to be.

"Why don't you come with me?" the doctor asked.

"I'd like to stay," Troy said. He felt a bizarre calmness. All the pain had been ripped away. This was more forceful than forgetting. He remembered everything. His soul was cut free. His body was a shell, a walking pod, nothing inside but the cold. The important parts were soaring up, now. Soaring up that straw shoved deep into the dirt—

"I can't have you in here, sir. Come with me. You'll freeze in here."

Troy glanced down. He had forgotten to put on shoes. He curled his toes away from the floor...then let them settle.

"Sir? Please." The young doctor gestured down the aisle. Troy let go of his own arm and saw that things were handled as needed. No kicking meant no straps. No shivering meant no shots.

He heard the squeak of hurrying boots out in the hallway. A large man from Security appeared by the open vault door, visibly winded. Troy caught a glimpse out of the corner of his eye of the doctor waving the man down. They were trying not to scare him. They didn't know that he couldn't be scared anymore. That part of him had drowned. Their medicine had killed it.

"You'll put me away for good," Troy said. It was something between a statement and a question. It was a realization. He wondered if he was like Hal—like *Carlton*—if the pills would never take again. He glanced toward the far end of the room, knew the empties were kept there. This was where he would be buried.

"Nice and easy," the doctor said.

He led Troy toward the exit; he would embalm him with that bright blue sky. The pods slid by as the two of them walked in silence.

The man from Security took deep breaths as he filled the doorway, his great chest heaving against his coveralls. There was a squeak from more boots as he was joined by another. Troy saw that his shift was over. Two weeks to go. He'd nearly made it.

The doctor waved the large men out of the way, seemed to hope they wouldn't be needed. They took up positions to either side; they seemed to think otherwise. Troy was led down the hallway, hope guiding him and fear flanking him.

"You *know*," Troy told the doctor, turning to study him. "You remember everything, don't you?"

The doctor didn't turn to face him. He simply nodded.

This felt like a betrayal. It wasn't fair.

"Why do you get to remember?" Troy asked. He wanted to know why those dispensing the medicine didn't have to take some of their own.

The doctor waved him into his office. His assistant was there, wearing a sleepshirt and hanging an IV bag bulging with blue. Troy had disturbed their sleep—just as they had once disturbed his.

"Some of us remember," the doctor said, "because we know this isn't a bad thing we've done." He frowned as he helped Troy onto the gurney. He seemed truly sad about Troy's condition. "We're doing good work, here," he said. "We're saving the world, not ending it. And the medicine only touches our regrets." He glanced up. "Some of us don't have any."

The doorway was stuffed with Security. It overflowed. The assistant unbuckled Troy's coveralls. Troy watched numbly.

"It would take a different kind of drug to touch what *we* know," the doctor said. He pulled a clipboard from the wall. A sheet of paper was fed into its jaws. There was a pause, a silent moment of comedic irony, and then a pen pressed into Troy's palm.

Troy laughed as he signed off on himself. This reminded him of his last job: the insane pretending to be sane, the world run from an asylum, a fetid swamp.

"Then why me?" he asked. "Why am I here?" He had always wanted to ask this of someone who might know. These were the prayers of youth, but now with a chance of some reply.

The doctor smiled and took the clipboard. He was probably in his late twenties. Troy was a handful of years shy of forty. And yet this man had all the wisdom, all the answers.

"It's good to have people like you in charge," the doctor said, and he seemed to genuinely mean it. The clipboard was returned to its peg. One of the Security men yawned and covered his mouth. Troy watched as his coveralls flopped to his waist. A fingernail makes a distinct click when it taps against a needle.

"I'd like to think about this," Troy said. He felt a sudden panic wash over him. He knew this needed to happen, but just five more minutes to think about it. Five more minutes alone with his thoughts, to savor this brief bout of comprehension. Five minutes before his brain was turned off. He wanted to sleep, certainly, but not quite yet.

The men in the doorway stirred as they sensed Troy's doubts, could see the fear in his eyes. The image of his boots slamming the gurney returned.

"I wish there was some other way," the doctor said sadly. He rested a hand on Troy's shoulder, guided him back against the table. The men from Security stepped closer. Their faces were sleepy, but Troy could tell they'd seen this before. They knew he was about to lash out, about to go mad.

There was a prick on his arm, a deep bite without warning. He looked down and saw the silver barb slide into his vein, the bright blue pumped inside.

"I don't want—" he said.

There were hands on his shins, his knees, weight on his shoulders. The heaviness against his chest was from something else.

A burning flowed through his body, chased immediately by numbness. They weren't putting him to sleep. *They were killing him.* Troy knew this as suddenly and swiftly as he knew that his wife was dead, that some other person had tried to take her place. He would go into a coffin *for good* this time. And all the dirt piled over his head would finally serve some purpose.

Darkness squeezed in around his vision. He closed his eyes, tried to yell for it to stop, but nothing came out. He wanted to kick and fight it, but more than mere hands had a hold of him, now. He was sinking. Cast off his own ship and into the cold waters. He would sink forever to the bottom. That's how long it would take for him to get there.

His last thoughts were of his beautiful wife, but the thoughts made little sense—it was the dreamworld invading.

*She's in Tennessee,* he thought. He didn't know why or how he knew this. But she was there—and waiting on him. She was already dead, had a spot hollowed out by her side, waiting.

Troy had just one more question, one name he hoped to grope for and seize before he went under, some part of himself to take with him to those deeps. It was on the tip of his tongue like a bitter pill, so close he could taste it—

But then he forgot.

# 23
## 2052 • Above Silo 1

The rain finally let up just as warring announcements and battling tunes filled the currents of air above the teeming hills. While the main stage was prepped for the evening's gala, it sounded to Donald as though the real action was taking place at all the other states. Opening bands ripped into their sets as the buzz of ATVs subsided to a trickle, all the busy little ants holing up in their nests.

It felt vaguely claustrophobic to be down in the bottom of the bowl by the Georgia stage. Donald felt an unquenchable urge for height, to be up on the ridge where he could see what was going on. It left him only imagining the sight of thousands of guests arrayed across each of the hills, picturing the political fervor in the air everywhere, the gelling of like-minded families celebrating the promise of something new.

As much as Donald wanted to celebrate new beginnings with them, he was mostly looking forward to the *end*. He couldn't wait for the convention to wrap up. The weeks had worn on him. He looked forward to no more stifling hot porta-potties with their chemical stench. No more meals neatly portioned out in little cardboard boxes with disposable plasticware in tiny baggies. No more bunking up in trailers that still smelled faintly of the men and women who had muddied Fulton County with their sweat and toil.

He was looking forward to a real bed, to some privacy, his computer, reliable cell phone service, dinners out, and most of all: time alone with his wife.

Fishing his cell phone out of his pocket, he checked his messages for the umpteenth time. They were minutes away from the anthem, from fifty stages blasting the same tune—for once, thank God—and then the flyover from the 141st. He had also heard someone mention fireworks to start the convention off with a bang. Donald worried they would be unimpressive unless they came after dusk.

His phone showed that the last half-dozen messages still hadn't gone through. The word *Sending* throbbed by each one, a circular arrow spinning around. He had plenty of bars—the network was just clogged. At least some of the earlier ones looked like they'd been sent. Helen would probably get the rest in a flood and think he'd lost his mind with worry. He scanned the wet banks for her, hoping to see her making her way down, arms out as she was careful with her balance, a smile he could spot from any distance.

Someone stepped up beside him. Donald looked away from the hills to see that Anna had joined him by the stage.

"Here we go," she said quietly, scanning the crowd.

She looked and sounded nervous. Maybe it was for her father, who had so much to do with arranging the main stage and making sure everyone was in the right place. Glancing back, he saw that people were taking their seats, chairs wiped down from the morning drizzle, not nearly as many people as it seemed before. They must be either working in the tents or off to the other stages. This was the quiet brewing before the—

"*There* she is."

Anna waved her arms. Donald felt his heart swell up into his neck as he turned and followed Anna's gaze. The relief was mixed with the panic of Helen seeing him there with her, the two of them waiting side by side.

Shuffling down the hill was certainly someone familiar. A young woman in a pressed blue uniform, a hat tucked under one arm, a dark head of hair wrapped up in a crisp bun.

"Charlotte?" Donald shielded his eyes from the glare of the noonday sun filtering through wispy clouds. He gaped in disbelief. All other events and concerns melted away as his sister spotted them and waved back.

"She sure as hell cut this close," Anna muttered.

Donald hurried over to his four-wheeler and turned the key. He hit the ignition, gave the handle some gas, and raced across the wet grass to meet her.

Charlotte beamed as he hit the brakes at the base of the hill. He killed the engine.

"Hey, Donny."

His sister leaned into him before he could dismount. She threw her arms around his neck and squeezed.

He returned her embrace, worried about denting or soiling her neat uniform. "What in the world are you doing here?" he asked.

She let go and took a step back, smoothed the front of her shirt. The gig line of her belt, pants, and top were all militarily straight. The Air Force dress hat disappeared back under her arm, every motion like an ingrained and precise habit.

"Are you surprised?" she asked. "I thought the Senator would've let it slip by now."

"Hell, no. Well, he said something about a visitor but not who. I thought you were in Iran. Did he swing this?"

She nodded, and Donald felt his cheeks cramping from smiling so hard. Every time he saw her, there was this relief from discovering that she was still the same person. The sharp chin and splash of freckles across her nose, the shine in her eyes that had not yet dulled from the horrible things she'd seen. She had just turned thirty, had been half a world away with no family when it happened, but she was frozen in his mind as the young teen who had enlisted, and it relieved him every time to see that she hadn't morphed into something else, not all the way.

"I think I'm supposed to be on the stage for this thing tonight," she said.

"Of course." Donald smiled. "I'm sure they'll want you on camera. You know, to show support for the troops."

Charlotte frowned. "Oh, God, I'm one of *those* people, aren't I?"

He laughed. "I'm sure they'll have someone from the Army, Navy, and Marines there with you."

"Oh, God. And I'm the *girl*."

They both laughed. One of the bands beyond the hills finished their set. The discordant mix of noise suddenly morphed into actual music as only one other stage was left performing. Donald scooted forward and told his sister to hop on, his chest suddenly less constricted. There had been a shift in the weather, these breaking clouds, the quieting stages, and now the arrival of family.

He cranked the engine and raced through the least muddy path on the way back to the stage, his sister holding on tight and squealing with delight. They pulled up beside Anna, his sister hopping off and into her arms. While they chatted, Donald killed the ignition and checked his phone. His messages were still sending. And then he saw that an incoming one had arrived.

Helen: *In Tennessee. where r u?*

There was a jarring moment as his brain tried to make sense of the message. It was from Helen. What the hell was she doing in *Tennessee*?

Another stage fell silent. It took only a heartbeat or two for Donald to realize that she wasn't hundreds of miles away. She was just over the hill. None of his messages about meeting at the Georgia stage had gone through.

"Hey, I'll be right back."

He cranked the ATV. Anna grabbed his wrist.

"Where are you going?" she asked.

He smiled. "Tennessee. Helen just texted me."

Anna glanced up at the clouds. His sister was inspecting her hat. On the stage, a young girl was being ushered up to the mic. She was flanked by a color guard, and the seats facing the stage were filling up, necks stretched with anticipation.

Before he could react or put it in gear, Anna reached across and twisted the key and pulled it out of the ignition.

"Not now," she said.

Donald felt a flash of rage. He reached for her hands, for the key, but it disappeared behind her back.

"Wait," she hissed.

Charlotte had turned toward the stage. Senator Thurman stood with a microphone in hand, the young girl, maybe sixteen, beside him. The hills had grown deathly quiet. Donald realized what a racket the ATV had been making. The girl was about to sing.

*Ladies and gentlemen, fellow Democrats—*

There was a pause. Donald got off the four-wheeler, took a last glance at his phone, then tucked it away.

*—and our handful of Independents.*

Laughter from the crowd. Donald set off at a jog across the flat at the bottom of the bowl. His shoes squished in the wet grass and the thin layer of mud. Senator Thurman's voice continued to roar through the microphone:

*Today is the dawn of a new era, a new time.*

He was out of shape. Or was his chest pounding from the time apart? From missing her and worrying all day? He flashed back to summer camp when he was a kid standing by the road with all the other kids, emotional farewells between new and supposedly eternal friends, but all he wanted was to see his mom and dad, to get home. He remembered nearly wetting his pants or bursting out in tears from trying to hold all the longing inside.

*As we gather in this place of future independence—*

By the time the ground sloped upward, he was already winded.

*—I'm reminded of the words from one of our enemies. A Republican.*

Distant laughter, but Donald was concentrating on the climb. The hill was steepest in a direct line toward the Tennessee bowl. Glancing to one side, he saw a crease in the hills where they had been pushed together, sealing up the path that once lay between them. That's how he should have gone.

*It was Ronald Reagan who once said that freedom must be fought for, that peace must be earned. As we listen to this anthem, written a long time ago as bombs dropped and a new country was forged, let's consider the price paid for our freedom and ask ourselves if any cost could be too great to ensure that these liberties never slip away.*

A third of the way up—and Donald had to stop and catch his breath. His calves were going to give out before his lungs did. He regretted puttering around on the ATV the past weeks while some of the others slogged it on foot. He promised himself he'd get in better shape.

He started back up the hill, and a voice like ringing crystal filled the bowl. It spilled in synchrony over the looming rise. He turned toward the stage below where the national anthem was being sung by the sweetest of young voices—

And he saw Anna hurrying up the hill after him, a scowl of worry on her face.

Donald knew he was in trouble. He wondered if he was dishonoring the anthem by scurrying up the hill. A few faces from the crowd were indeed trained his way. Everyone had assigned places for the anthem and he was ignoring his. He turned his back on the scowls and Anna both and set off with renewed resolve.

*—o'er the ramparts we watched—*

He laughed, out of breath, wondering if these mounds of earth could be considered ramparts. It was easy to see the bowls for what they'd become in the last weeks, individual states full of people, goods, and livestock, fifty state fairs bustling at once, all for this shining day, all to be gone once the facility began to operate according to its true purpose.

*—and the rockets' red glare, the bombs bursting in air—*

He reached the top of the hill and sucked in deep lungfuls of crisp, clean air. On the stage below, flags swayed idly in a soft breeze. A large screen showed a video of the girl singing about *proof* and *still being there.*

A hand seized his wrist. A fierce hand.

"Come back," Anna hissed.

He was panting. Anna was also out of breath, her knees covered in mud and grass stains. She must've slipped on the way up. He wondered if the anger in her voice and her narrowed eyes were related.

"Helen doesn't know where I am," he said.

*—bannerrr still waaaaave—*

Applause stirred before the end, a compliment. The jets streaking in from the distance caught his eye even before their rumble arrived. A diamond pattern with wingtips nearly touching.

"Get the fuck back down here," Anna yelled. She yanked on his arm.

Donald twisted his wrist away. He was mesmerized by the sight of the jets approaching.

*—o'er the laaand of the freeeeeee—*

That sweet and youthful voice lifted up from fifty holes in

the earth and crashed into the thunderous roar of the powerful jets, those soaring and graceful angels of death.

"Let go," Donald demanded, as Anna grabbed him and scrambled to pull him back down the hill.

*—and the hooome of the...braaaaave...*

Miles of applause bubbled up together. The air shook from the grumble of the perfectly timed fly-by. Afterburners screamed as the jets peeled apart and curved upward into the white clouds.

Anna was practically wrestling him, arms wrapped around his shoulders. Donald snapped out of a trance induced by the passing jets, the beautiful rendition of the anthem amplified across half a county, the struggle to spot his wife in the bowl below.

"Goddamnit, Donny, we've got to get *down—*"

The first flash came before she could get her hands over his eyes. A bright spot in the corner of his vision in the direction of downtown Atlanta. It was a daytime strike of lightning. Donald turned toward it, expecting thunder. The flash of light had become a blinding glow. Anna's arms were around his waist, jerking him backward. His sister was there, panting, covering her eyes, screaming *What the fuck?*

Another pop of light like being punched in the face, starbursts in one's vision. Sirens spilled out of all the speakers, a grating noise compared to the sweet voice they replaced. It was the recorded sound of air raid klaxons.

Donald felt half blinded. Even when the mushroom clouds rose up from the earth—impossibly large to be so distant—it still took a heartbeat to figure out what was going on.

They pulled him down the hill. Applause had turned to screams audible over the rise and fall of the blaring siren. Donald could hardly see. He stumbled backward and nearly fell as the three of them slipped and slid down the bowl, the wet grass funneling them toward the stage. The puffy tops of the swelling mushrooms rose up higher and higher, staying in sight even as the rest of the hills and the trees disappeared from view.

"Wait!" he yelled.

There was something he was forgetting. He couldn't remember what. He had an image of his ATV sitting up on the ridge. He was leaving it behind. How did he get up there? What was happening?

"Go. Go. Go." Anna was saying.

His sister was cussing. She was frightened and confused, just like him. He had never known his sister to be either one.

"The main tent!"

Donald spun around, his heels slipping in the grass, hands wet with rain and studded with mud and grass. When had he fallen?

The three of them tumbled down the last of the slope as the sound of distant thunder finally reached them. The clouds overhead seemed to race away from the blasts, pushed aside by an unnatural wind. The undersides of the clouds strobed and flashed as if more strikes of lightning were hitting, more bombs detonating. The air growled with the force of the earlier blows. Down by the stage, people weren't running to escape the bowl—they were instead flowing into tents, guided by volunteers with waving arms, the markets and food stalls clearing out, the rows of wooden chairs now a heaped and upturned tangle, a dog still tied to a post, barking.

Some people still seemed to be aware, to have their faculties intact. Anna was one of them. Donald saw the Senator by a smaller tent coordinating the flow of traffic. Where was everyone going? Donald felt disembodied as he was ushered along with the others. It took long moments for his brain to process what he'd seen. Nuclear blasts. The live view of what had forever been resigned to grainy wartime video. Real bombs going off in the real air. Nearby. He had seen them. Why wasn't he completely blind? Was that even what happened?

The raw fear of death overtook him. Donald knew, in some recess of his mind, that they were all dead. The end of all things was coming. There was no outrunning it. No hiding. Paragraphs from a book he'd read came to mind, thousands of paragraphs memorized. He patted his pants for his pills, but they weren't there. Looking over his shoulder, he fought to remember what he'd left behind—

Anna and his sister pulled him past the Senator, who wore a hard scowl of determination, who frowned at his daughter. The tent flap brushed Donald's face, the darkness within interspersed with a few hanging lights. The spots in his vision from the blasts made themselves known in the blackness. There was a crush of people, but not as many as there should have been. Where were the crowds? It didn't make sense until he found himself shuffling downward.

A concrete ramp, bodies on all sides, shoulders jostling, people wheezing, yelling for one another, hands outstretched as the flowing crush drove loved ones away, husband and wife separated, some people crying, some perfectly poised—

Husband and wife.

Helen!

Donald heard her name over the crowd. But it was his voice. He was yelling it. He turned and tried to swim against the flowing torrent of the frightened. Anna and his sister pulled on him. People fighting to get below pushed from above. Donald was forced to move the opposite direction of his feet, of his will. He was drowning. The tide was pulling him beneath the waves, a white mist rising up around him like sea foam. He wanted to go under with his wife. He wanted to drown with her.

*"Helen!"*

Oh, God, he remembered.

He remembered what he had left behind.

Panic subsided and fear took its place. He could see. His vision had cleared. But he could not swim up the ramp, could not fight the push of the inevitable. His world was gone.

Donald remembered a conversation with the Senator about how it would all end. There was an electricity in the air, the taste of dead metal on his tongue. He remembered most of a book. He knew what this was, what was happening.

His world was gone.

A new one swallowed him.

*In 2007, the Center for Automation in Nanobiotech (CAN) outlined the hardware and software platform that would one day allow robots smaller than human cells to make medical diagnoses, conduct repairs, and even self-propagate.*

*In the same year, the CBS network re-aired a program about the effects of propranolol on sufferers of extreme trauma. A simple pill, it had been discovered, could wipe out the memory of any traumatic event.*

*At almost the same moment in humanity's broad history, mankind had discovered the means for bringing about its utter downfall. And the ability to forget it ever happened.*

# Epilogue

Troy startled awake from a series of terrible dreams. The world was on fire, and the people who had been sent to put it out were all asleep. Asleep and frozen stiff, smoking matches still in their hands, wisps and gray curls of evil deeds.

He had been buried, was enveloped in darkness, could feel the tight walls of his small coffin like a closed fist.

The confinement brought a scream to his lips, but his fearful cries leaked out in a trembling whimper.

Dark shapes moved beyond the frosted glass, the men with their shovels trying to free him.

Troy's eyelids seemed to rip and crack as he fought to open them fully. There was crust in the corners of them, melting frost coursing down his cheek. He tried to lift his arms to wipe it away, but they responded feebly. An IV tugged at his wrist as he managed to raise one hand. He was aware of his catheter. Every inch of his body tingled as he emerged from the numbness and into the cold.

The lid popped with a hiss of air. There was a crack of light to his side that grew as the suffocating shadows folded away.

A doctor and his assistant reached in to tend to him. Troy remembered this. This was real. So were the nightmares. He tried to speak but could only cough. They helped him up, brought him the bitter drink. Swallowing took effort. His hands were so weak, arms trembling, they had to help him with the cup. The taste on his tongue was metallic. It tasted like the death of a machine.

"Easy," they said when he tried to drink too fast. Tubes and IVs were carefully removed by expert hands, pressure applied, gauze taped to frigid skin. There was a paper gown. He remembered this.

"What year?" he asked, his voice a dry rasp.

"It's early," the doctor said, a different doctor. Troy blinked against the harsh lights, didn't recognize either man tending to him. The sea of coffins around him remained a hazy blur.

"Take your time," the assistant said, tilting the cup.

Troy managed a few sips. He felt worse than last time. It had been longer. The cold was deep within his bones. He remembered that his name wasn't Troy. He was supposed to be dead. Part of him regretted being disturbed. Another part hoped he had slept through the worst of it.

"Sir, we're sorry to wake you, but we need your help."

"Your report—"

Both men were talking at once.

"Another silo is having problems, sir. Silo 18—"

Pills were produced. Troy waved them away. He no longer wished to take them.

The doctor hesitated, the two capsules of clear blue sky resting in his palm. He turned to consult with someone else, a third man. Troy tried to blink the world into focus. Something was said. Fingers curled around the pills, filling him with relief.

They helped him up, had a wheelchair waiting. A man stood behind it, his hair as stark white as his coveralls, his square jaw and iron frame familiar. Troy recognized him. This was the man who woke the freezing.

Another sip of water as he leaned against the pod, knees trembling from the weak and cold.

"What *about* Silo 18?" Troy whispered the question as the cup was lowered.

The doctor frowned and said nothing. The man behind the wheelchair studied him intently.

"I know you," Troy said.

The man in white nodded. The wheelchair was waiting for Troy. His sleep had been longer, his legs more like a newborn's than a foal's. Troy felt his stomach twist as dormant parts of him stirred.

"You're the Thaw Man," he said, even though this didn't sound quite right.

The paper gown was warm. It rustled like the leaves of winter as his arms were guided through the sleeves. The men working on him were nervous. They chattered back and forth, one of them saying a silo was falling, the other that they needed his help. Troy only cared about the man in white. They helped him toward the wheelchair.

"Is it over?" he asked. He watched the colorless man, his vision clearing, his voice growing stronger. He dearly hoped that he had slept through it all.

The Thaw Man shook his head sadly. Troy was lowered into the chair.

"I'm afraid, son," a familiar voice said, "that it's only begun."

www.hughhowey.com

Made in the USA
San Bernardino, CA
25 November 2012